## 'You do real

'Yes,' she surprise
her voice was tren gone
all smoky.

'I will never fall in love with you,' he added,
even as his hands slipped inside her jacket.

'I don't expect you to,' she replied somewhat
breathlessly.

'You don't have to do anything you don't want
to do,' he told her, before his conscience shut
down entirely.

'But I want you to,' she choked out.

'Want me to do what?' he murmured, as he
slipped the jacket off her shoulders and let it
fall to the carpet.

'Wh-whatever,' she stammered.

Any hope of salvation fled. He was lost and so,
he realised when he looked down into her
dilating eyes, was she…

**Miranda Lee** is Australian, living near Sydney. Born and raised in the bush, she was boarding-school-educated and briefly pursued a career in classical music, before moving to Sydney and embracing the world of computers. Happily married, with three daughters, she began writing when family commitments kept her at home. She likes to create stories that are believable, modern, fast-paced and sexy. Her interests include meaty sagas, doing word puzzles, gambling and going to the movies.

**Recent titles by the same author:**

A SECRET VEGEANCE*
THE SECRET LOVE-CHILD*

*Secret Passions

# AT HER BOSS'S BIDDING

BY
MIRANDA LEE

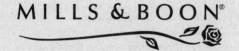

MILLS & BOON®

*First published in Great Britain 2002*
*Harlequin Mills & Boon Limited,*
*Eton House, 18-24 Paradise Road, Richmond, Surrey TW9 1SR*

© Miranda Lee 2002

ISBN 0 263 83198 1

*Set in Times Roman 10½ on 12 pt.*
*01-0103-46410*

*Printed and bound in Spain*
*by Litografía Rosés, S.A., Barcelona*

## PROLOGUE

SHE was perfect, Justin thought from the first moment Ms Rachel Witherspoon walked in to be interviewed.

Perfectly plain and prim-looking, dressed in a very unsexy black suit, mousy brown hair severely scraped back and anchored in a twist. No make-up and no perfume, he realised with relief, the absolute opposite of the blonde bombshell who'd been wiggling her way around his office for the last month, pretending to be his personal assistant.

No, that was probably unfair. The girl had been efficient enough. The company who'd sent her over straight away after his previous PA quit on short notice didn't have dummies on their books.

But she'd made it clear within a few days that her services could easily extend beyond being just his PA. She'd used every opportunity—and every weapon in her considerable physical arsenal—to get this message across. He'd been bombarded with provocative clothes, provocative smiles and provocative comments till he couldn't bear another second. When she'd come in last Monday, showing more cleavage than a call-girl, Justin had cracked.

He didn't sack her as such. He didn't have to. She was just a temp. He simply told her that this would be her last week, saying that he'd hired a permanent PA and she was starting the following Monday.

A lie, of course. But a necessary one for his sanity.

Not that he was sexually tempted by her. Oh, no. It

5

was just that every time she came on to him, he was reminded of Mandy and what she must have got up to with that boss of hers. What she was *still* getting up to every single day, jet-setting around the world and being his personal assistant in every which way there was.

Justin's jaw clenched down hard at the thought. It had been eighteen months since his wife had confessed what had been going on, then added the shattering news that she was leaving him to become her boss's mistress.

Eighteen months! Yet the pain was still there. The pain of her betrayal and deception, plus the sharpest memory of the hurtful things she'd said to him that final day. Cruel things. Soul-destroying things!

Most men who'd been so savagely dumped might have soothed their battered egos by going out and bedding every female in sight. But Justin hadn't been to bed with a single woman since Mandy walked out. He simply hadn't wanted to. Just the thought of being physically intimate with another female made him shudder.

Of course, none of his male friends and colleagues knew that. You didn't confess such things to other men. They would never understand, or sympathise. His mother had an inkling, though. She knew how hurt he'd been by Mandy's deception and desertion. She kept telling him that someday he'd meet a really nice woman who'd make him forget about Mandy.

Mothers were eternal optimists. And incorrigible matchmakers.

So when his mum—to whom he'd been complaining about his office situation—rang last weekend to say that she had the perfect PA for him he'd been understandably wary. Only after he'd struggled without a secretary for a week, and been repeatedly reassured that this Rachel was nothing like his temptation of a temp, did Justin agree to interview Ms Witherspoon.

And here she was. In the flesh.

What there was of it.

She was so thin! And terribly tired-looking, with huge black rings under her eyes. Nice eyes, though. Nice shape. And an interesting colour. But so sad.

She was supposed to be only thirty-one, according to the birthdate on her résumé. But she looked closer to forty.

Understandable, he supposed, after what she'd gone through these last few years. Sympathy for her washed through Justin and he decided then and there to offer her the job. He already knew she had the qualifications, even if she might be a bit rusty. But someone as smart as she obviously was would have no trouble brushing up on her secretarial skills.

Still, he supposed he had to go through the motions of a proper interview, otherwise she might think it a bit fishy. Nobody liked charity. Or pity.

'So, Rachel,' he said matter-of-factly once she'd settled herself in the chair. 'My mother has told me a lot about you. And your résumé here is very impressive,' he added, tapping the two-page work history which had been faxed to him the day before. 'I see you were finalist in the Secretary of the Year competition a few years back. And your boss at that time was very high up in the Australian Broadcasting Corporation. Perhaps you could tell me a little about your work experience there...'

# CHAPTER ONE

'THIS is just like old times, isn't it?' Rachel said to Isabel as she jumped into bed and pulled the pretty patchwork quilt up to her chin.

'True,' Isabel returned, and climbed into the matching single bed, her memory racing back to those old times.

Rachel and Isabel had attended the same boarding-school, and become best friends from day one. After Rachel's parents were killed in a freak train accident when Rachel was only fourteen, the girls had grown even closer. When Rachel's upbringing had been taken over by her mother's best friend, a nice lady named Lettie, Isabel had been thrilled to discover that Lettie lived in the same suburb of Sydney as her parents did. During the school holidays Rachel had often slept over at Isabel's. Sometimes, she'd stayed for days. Lettie hadn't minded. The girls had become inseparable, and liked nothing better than to lie awake in bed at night and talk for hours.

Rachel smiled over at Isabel. 'I feel like fifteen again.'

Well, you don't *look* like fifteen, Isabel thought with an inner sigh. Rachel looked every one of her thirty-one years, and then some. Which was a real pity. She'd once been drop-dead gorgeous, with glossy auburn hair, flashing eyes and a fab figure which Isabel had always envied.

But four years of nursing her terminally ill foster-

8

mother had taken its toll. Rachel was a mere shadow of her former self.

Isabel had hoped that Lettie's finally passing away— the poor love had been suffering from Alzheimer's— and Rachel getting back into the workforce would put some oomph back into the girl.

But that hadn't happened yet.

Still, it had only been a few weeks.

She *had* put on a couple of pounds, which was a start. And when she smiled as she had just then you could catch a glimpse of the vibrant beauty she'd once been.

Hopefully, tomorrow, at the wedding, she'd smile a lot. Otherwise, when she saw the photographs of herself at a later date she'd be in for a shock. Isabel knew that she herself was looking her very best. Love suited her. As did pregnancy.

She was glowing.

Isabel was glad now that she'd taken *some* measures to make sure her chief bridesmaid didn't suffer too much by comparison.

'Promise me you'll let my hairdresser have his wicked way with you tomorrow,' Isabel insisted. 'Red hair will look much better with your turquoise dress than brown. And its bare neckline needs curls bouncing around on your shoulders. None of that wearing your hair pulled back like you do for work. Or up in any way. Rafe hates hair worn up on a woman, anyway. I've also hired a make-up artist to do our faces and I don't want to hear any objections.'

'I won't object. It's your day. I'll do whatever you want. But just a temporary rinse in my hair, please. I don't want to show up at the office on Monday morning with red hair.'

'Why not?'

'You know why not. One of the reasons Justin hired me as his PA was because I was nothing like my predecessor. She'd been flashy and flirtatious, remember? Alice told us all about her.'

Isabel rolled her eyes. 'I don't think a bit of red dye in your hair constitutes flashy and flirtatious.'

'Maybe not, but I don't want to take any chances. I like my job, Isabel. I don't want to do anything to risk losing it.'

'You know, when I first heard about Justin McCarthy I thought he was being sensible, not wanting a glamour-puss secretary who obviously had the hots for him. Office affairs rarely end well, especially for the woman. Now I'm beginning to agree more with Rafe's opinion of him. He says any divorced guy who fires a beautiful PA for flirting with him has to either be paranoid about women, or gay.'

'He did not fire my predecessor,' Rachel said, rather defensively, Isabel thought. 'She was just a temp. And Justin is not at all paranoid about women. He's very nice to me.'

'You said he was difficult and demanding.'

Rachel sighed. 'That was only on the day I somehow stupidly deleted a file and it took him six hours to recover it. Normally, he's very even-tempered.'

'Not all bitter and twisted?'

'I don't see any evidence of it.'

'OK, that leaves gay. So, what do you think? Is your boss gay? Could that be the reason his wife left him?'

'I honestly don't know, and quite frankly, Isabel, I don't care. My boss's private life is his own business.'

'But you said he was good-looking. And only in his

mid-thirties. Are you saying you're not attracted to him, just a little?'

'Not at all. *No*,' Rachel repeated firmly when Isabel gave her a long, narrowed-eyed look.

'I don't believe you. You told me a little while back that you were so lonely you'd sleep with anything in trousers. Now here you are, working very closely with a handsome hunk of possibly heterosexual flesh and you're telling me you don't have the occasional sexual fantasy about him? You might be a bit depressed, Rach, but you're not dead. This is me you're talking to, remember? Your best friend. Your confidante in matters up close and personal over the years. I haven't forgotten that you lost your virginity at the tender age of sixteen, and you were never without a boyfriend after that till Eric dumped you. You might not like men much any more, given what that bastard did, but—'

'Oh, I still like *some* men,' Rachel broke in. 'I like Rafe,' she added with a cheeky little grin.

'Yes, well, all females like Rafe,' Isabel returned drily, 'even my mother. But since darling Rafe is already the father of my babe-to-be, and about to become my husband tomorrow, then you can't have him, not even on loan. You'll have to find some other hunk to see to your sexual needs.'

'Who said I had sexual needs?'

'Don't you?' Isabel was startled. She must have after four years of celibacy!

'I don't seem to. I rarely *think* about sex any more, let alone need it.'

Yes, that was patently obvious, now that Isabel came to think about it. If Rachel felt like sex occasionally, she'd do herself up a bit, and to hell with her paranoid boss. There were plenty of other secretarial jobs in the

world, and plenty of other men to go with them. The
business district of Sydney was full of very attractive
men of all ages. Of course, with her looks on the wane,
Rachel might not be able to catch herself a seriously
gorgeous hunk like Rafe, but there was no reason for
her to be lonely, or celibate.

'Actually, I'm not sure I ever did need it, as such,'
Rachel went on thoughtfully. 'Sex was just another
facet of my being in love. Losing my virginity at sixteen wasn't a sexual urge so much as an emotional one.
I'd fallen in love for the first time and I wanted to give
myself to Josh.'

'But you enjoyed it. You told me so.'

'Yes, I certainly did. But it wasn't just sex I was
after. It was that lovely feeling of being loved.'

Isabel smiled. 'You know, it's possible to have very
good sex without love, Rach.'

'Maybe for you, but not for me. When I said I'd
sleep with anyone after Lettie died, that was just my
grief and loneliness talking. I can't just sleep with anyone. I have to be in love and, quite frankly, since my
experience with Eric I don't think I'm capable of falling in love any more. I just don't have the heart for it.
Or the courage. Eric hurt me more than I could ever
explain. I honestly thought he loved me as much as I
loved him. But, looking back, I don't think he loved
me at all.'

'He didn't, the selfish rat. But that doesn't mean that
one day you won't meet a man who will love you the
way you deserve to be loved.'

'You're only saying that because you were lucky
enough to find Rafe. Not so long ago, you didn't have
such a high opinion of the male sex.'

'True.' Isabel couldn't deny that she'd been a classic

cynic for ages where men were concerned. She'd spent most of her adult female life falling in love with Mr Wrong. She knew where Rachel was coming from and, honestly, she couldn't blame her for feeling the way she did. Eric had treated her shamefully, dumping her after he found out Rachel was quitting her job to look after Lettie. That, coming on top of Lettie's own husband heartlessly abandoning his increasingly vague wife, must have been the final straw. It was no wonder Rachel's faith in the male sex had been seriously dented.

'I'm quite happy as I am, Isabel,' Rachel went on, '*without* a man in my personal life. I'm really enjoying my job. It's very interesting working for an investment consultant. I'm learning a lot about the stock market, and money matters, which hasn't exactly been my forte till now, as you know. I'm thinking of going to university at night next year and doing a business degree, part-time. I have plans for my life, Isabel, so don't you worry about me. I'll be fine.'

Isabel sighed. That's what she always said. Rachel was one brave girl. But a rather unlucky one. When Lettie died they'd both thought she'd at least have some financial equity in Lettie's house, despite it being mortgaged. Rachel was the sole beneficiary in Lettie's will, made after Lettie's husband had deserted her. Rachel had been going to sell the house and put a deposit on an inner-city apartment with the money left over after the loan had been repaid. So she'd been shattered to find out the house was still in Lettie's husband's name.

When Rachel went to the solicitor who was looking after Lettie's estate and explained that she'd personally paid the mortgage for the past four and a half years with money she'd earned doing clothes alterations at home, the solicitor had countered that Lettie's ex had paid the mortgage for fifteen years before that and had no intention of giving her a cent.

She was also informed that Lettie's ex was thinking of contesting Lettie's last will as well, since it was made after she was diagnosed with a mentally debilitating illness. Rachel was advised she could go to court to fight for a share of the house and contents if she wished, but her case was shaky. Even if she won, the amount of money she'd be awarded would undoubtedly be exceeded by her court costs.

So Rachel had walked away with nothing but a few personal possessions, her clothes and a second-hand sewing machine.

She'd temporarily been living with Isabel in her town house at Turramurra, and had agreed to house-sit whilst Isabel and Rafe were away on their honeymoon. Isabel had offered her the use of her place on a permanent basis for a nominal rent, since she was moving into Rafe's inner-city terraced house on their return, but Rachel had refused, saying she would look for a small place of her own closer to the city.

Silly, really, Isabel thought. She should let her friends help her in her hour of need. But that was Rachel for you. Independent and proud. *Too* proud.

But the nicest person in the world.

Isabel hoped that one day a man might come along worthy of her. A man of character and sensitivity. A man with a lot of love to give.

Because of course that was what Rachel needed. To be loved. Truly. Madly. Deeply.

Just as Rafe loves me, Isabel thought dreamily.

God, she was so lucky.

Poor Rachel. She did feel terribly sorry for her.

# CHAPTER TWO

RACHEL hurried down the city street the following Monday morning, anxious not to be late for work. She'd caught a slightly later train than usual, courtesy of the longer time it had taken her to get ready for work that morning. Now she was trying to make up for lost time, her sensibly shod feet working hard.

Turning a corner into a city street which faced east, Rachel was suddenly confronted by the rays of the rising sun slanting straight into her eyes. But she didn't slacken her pace.

The day was going to be warm again, she quickly realised. Too warm, really, for a black suit with a long-sleeved jacket. Spring had been late coming to Sydney this year, but it was now here with a vengeance. October had had record temperatures so far and today looked like no exception. Not a cloud marred the clear blue sky, making the weather forecast for a southerly change today highly unlikely.

There was no doubt about it. She'd have to buy some new work clothes soon. What she'd been wearing would not take her right through the spring till summer. She should never have been stupid enough to buy all long-sleeved suits to begin with. She'd buy something other than black next time too, though nothing bright or frivolous. Something which would go with black accessories. Light grey, perhaps. Or camel. That colour was very in.

Unfortunately, such shopping would have to wait till

Isabel got home from her honeymoon in three weeks' time. Rachel didn't have a clue where the shops were that Isabel had taken her to last time, and which catered brilliantly for the serious career girl. Admittedly, a large percentage of the clothes in those shops was black, but they also had other colours.

Till then, however, she was stuck with black. And long sleeves.

Thank heaven for air-conditioning, she thought as she pushed the sleeves up her arms and puffed her way up the increasingly steep incline.

A sideways glance at her reflection in a shop window brought a groan to her lips. Her hair was still red, despite several washings yesterday and a couple more this morning. Maybe not quite as bright a red as it had been for the wedding on Saturday, but bright enough. She wished now she'd gone out yesterday and bought a brown hair dye. But at the time she'd been hoping the colour would still wash out.

If Isabel hadn't already been winging her way overseas on her honeymoon, Rachel would have torn strips off her mischief-making best friend. That hairdresser of hers must have used a semi-permanent colour on her hair, Rachel was sure of it.

Admittedly, she'd ended up looking pretty good for the wedding. From a distance. Amazing what a glamorous dress, a big hairdo and a make-up expert could achieve. But that was then and this was now, and bright red hair did not sit well with Rachel's normally un-made-up face, or her decidedly *un*-glamorous work wardrobe.

She was thankful that the repeated washings yesterday had toned down the colour somewhat. Hopefully, the way she was wearing it today—scraped back even more severely than usual—would also minimise the effect. She would hate for Justin to think that she was suddenly trying to attract his attention in any way.

As she'd told Isabel the other night, she liked her job. And she didn't want to lose it. Or even remotely risk the good relationship she'd already established with her boss, which was very professional and based on mutual respect. Justin had told her only last week what a relief it was to come into work and not be overpowered by some cloying perfume, or confronted with a cleavage deep enough to lose the Harbour Bridge in.

Rachel was out of breath by the time she reached the tall city office block which housed the huge insurance company where she worked.

When she'd first heard about the job as Justin's PA Rachel had been under the impression that Justin was an AWI executive. That wasn't the case, however. He was an independent hot-shot financial analyst under contract to AWI to give them his exclusive financial advice for two years, after which Justin planned on starting up his own consultancy company. Preferably in an office away from the inner-city area, he'd explained to her one day over a mutual coffee break, ideally overlooking one of the northern beaches.

Meanwhile, AWI had given him use of a suite of rooms on the fifteenth floor of their building, which was high up enough to have a good view of the city and the harbour.

But the view wasn't the only good thing about this suite of rooms. The space was incredible. Rachel had sole occupancy of the entire reception area, which was huge, and boasted its own powder room and tea-cum-store room, along with a massive semicircular work station where three secretaries could have happily worked side by side without being cramped.

Justin's office beyond was just as spacious, as well as having two large adjoining rooms, one furnished for meetings, the other for relaxing and entertaining. Rachel had never seen a better-stocked bar, not to mention such a lavish bathroom, tiled from top to bottom in black marble, with the most exquisite gold fittings.

Justin had confided to her during her first interview that this suite of rooms had previously been occupied by an AWI superannuation-fund manager who'd redecorated as if he owned the company, and been subsequently sacked. No expense had been spared, from the plush sable carpet to the sleekly modern beech office furniture, the Italian cream leather sofas and the impressionistic art originals on the walls.

Clearly, Justin being allotted this five-star suite of rooms showed how much his skills were valued by his temporary employers.

Rachel valued him as her boss, too. She admired his strong work ethics and his lack of personal arrogance. Most men with his looks and intelligence possessed egos to match. Justin didn't. Not that he was perfect, by any means. He did have his difficult and demanding moments. And some days his mood left a lot to be desired.

Still, Rachel already knew she'd like nothing better than to go with him when he left to set up his own company. He'd already implied she could, if she wanted to. He seemed as pleased with her as she was with him.

A shaft of sunshine lit up Rachel's red hair again as she pushed her way into the building's foyer through the revolving glass doors. The top of her head fairly glowed in the glass and she groaned again. She would definitely be going out at lunch time and buying that brown dye. Meanwhile, she would explain to Justin the reason behind her change of hair colour, and that it was as good as gone. Then he couldn't jump to any wrong conclusions.

No one gave Rachel a second glance during the lift ride up to the fifteenth floor, which was because none of the smartly dressed men and women in the lift even knew her. Few people who worked in the building knew her. Justin worked alone, with only the occasional fund manager actually dropping in for advice, face to face. Mostly they contacted Justin by phone or email, and vice versa.

So far, he hadn't held a single meeting around the boardroom-like table in his meeting room, and only once to her knowledge had he entertained an AWI executive in the other room. Sometimes, he had a nap in there on one of the two sofas after he'd been working all night. He did attend monthly meetings upstairs with all the fund managers, but he never attended the company's social functions, and he resolutely refused to become involved in AWI's internal politics.

The truth was her boss was a loner.

Which suited Rachel just fine.

She'd found that since her lengthy stay-at-home absence from the workforce—and the outside world in general—she'd become a bit agoraphobic. She liked the insular security of her present office situation, plus the little contact with strangers which her working day held. She no longer seemed to have the confidence she'd once had to make small talk with lots of people. She'd actually become quite shy, except with her very close friends, like Isabel and Rafe, which wasn't like her at all. She'd once had a very outgoing personality.

Isabel kept saying she'd get back to her old self eventually.

But Rachel was beginning to doubt it. Her experiences over the last few years had definitely changed her. She'd become introverted. And serious. And, yes, plain.

That was one of the biggest changes in her, of course. She'd lost her looks. And dying her hair red wasn't going to get them back. All it made her feel was foolish.

The lift doors opened and Rachel bolted down the corridor, hopeful of still arriving before Justin. He worked out in the company gym every day before work, and occasionally lost track of time. Hence his tardy arrival at the office on the odd morning.

The door from the corridor was still locked, heralding that this was one of those mornings. Rachel sighed with relief as she found her key, already planning in her mind to be sitting at her desk, looking coolly composed and beavering away on her computer when Justin finally came in.

She was doing just that when the door burst open fifteen minutes later. Her heart did jump, but not for any sexually charged reason, as Isabel had fantasised the other night, just instant agitation. What would her boss say when he saw her hair?

Justin strode in, looking his usual attractive but conservative self in a navy pinstriped suit, white shirt and bland blue tie. His damp dark hair was slicked back at the sides, indicating that he'd not long showered. He had the morning papers tucked under one arm and was carrying his black briefcase in the other. He was frowning, though not at her, his deeply set blue eyes quite distracted, his thick dark brows drawn together over his strong, straight nose in an attitude of worried concentration.

'Morning, Rachel,' he said with only the briefest sidewards glance as he hurried past. 'Hold the coffee for ten minutes, would you?' he tossed over his shoulder as he forged on into his private sanctuary. 'I have something I have to do first.'

When he banged the door shut behind him Rachel glared after him, her hazel eyes showing some feminine pique for once.

'Well!' she huffed at the closed door. 'And good morning to you, too!'

So much for his having noticed her red hair. It came to Rachel that she could have been sitting there stark naked this morning, and Justin would not have noticed.

Not that her being naked was anything to write home about these days. Despite having put on a couple of pounds during the past month, she was still thin, her once noteworthy breasts having long ago shrunk from a voluptuous D-cup to a very average B plus. She'd complained about it to Isabel on Saturday when they were getting dressed before the wedding.

'You still have bigger boobs than me,' Isabel returned as she surveyed Rachel in her underwear. 'OK, so you're thin, but you're in proportion. Actually, you look darned good in the buff, girl. You've surprised me.'

Rachel had laughed at the time. She laughed now, but with a different type of self-mockery. What on earth was she doing, even thinking about what she looked like naked? Who cared? No one was going to see her that way, except herself.

Again, it was all Isabel's fault, putting silly thoughts into her head about Justin and sex.

Sex! Now, that was a subject not worth thinking about.

So why was she suddenly thinking about it?

Rachel filled in the next eight minutes trying to work through her irritability, before giving up and rising to go pour Justin a mug of coffee from the coffee maker, which she kept perking all day. Justin liked his coffee. She figured that ten minutes would have passed by the time she carried it in to him. Any further delay was unacceptable. The sooner he noticed her red hair, and the sooner she explained the reason behind it, the sooner she'd be able to settle down to work, and put aside the fear of looking ludicrous in her boss's eyes.

'Come in,' Justin snapped when she tapped on his office door exactly ten minutes after his order.

She entered to find him sitting at the bank of computers which lined the far side of his U-shaped work station. His back remained to her as he rode his swivel chair down the long line of computers, peering at each screen for a couple of seconds as he went. His jacket was off and his shirtsleeves rolled up. His tie, she knew without being able to see it, would be loosened.

As Rachel made her way across the room Justin slid down in front of the furthest computer on the right.

'Just put it down here,' he directed, patting an empty spot next to his right elbow without looking up.

Grimacing with frustration, Rachel put the coffee down where ordered and was about to leave when she stopped.

'Justin…'

'Mmm?'

He still didn't look up.

She sighed. 'Justin, I need to talk to you,' she said firmly.

'What about?' Again, no eye contact.

'I wanted to explain to you about my red hair.'

'What red hair?' He spun round from the computer, his eyes finally lifting. He frowned up at her, his head tipping slightly to one side. 'Mmm. It's a bit bright for you, isn't it?'

Rachel winced. 'It looked all right for the wedding on Saturday,' she said, her pride demanding she say something in her own defence.

His blue eyes widened. 'Wedding? What wedding? My God, Rachel, you didn't go and get married on the weekend without telling me, did you?'

Rachel almost laughed. As if.

'I don't think you need worry about that ever happening, Justin,' she said drily. 'No, I was a bridesmaid at my best friend's wedding on Saturday and she insisted on having my hair dyed red for the day. It was supposed to wash out afterwards but, as you can see, it didn't. I just wanted to reassure you that I'm going to dye it back to brown tonight.'

He shrugged his indifference, then picked up his coffee. 'Why bother?' he said between sips. 'It doesn't look *that* bad. And it'll wash out—or grow out—eventually.'

Rachel's shoulders stiffened. It would take two years for it to grow out. Did he honestly think she had such little personal pride that she'd walk around with half-red, half-brown hair for two *years*?

Clearly, he did.

'It looks dreadful and you know it,' she said sharply, and whirled away from him before she did something she would regret.

Rachel could feel him staring after her as she marched towards the open doorway, probably wondering what was wrong with her. She'd never spoken to him in that tone before. But when she turned to close the door behind her he wasn't staring after her at all. Or even thinking about her. He was back, peering at the maze of figures on the computer, her red hair—plus her slight outburst—clearly forgotten.

Rachel didn't realise the extent of her anger till she tried to get back to work. Why she was so angry with Justin, she couldn't understand. His indifferent reaction to her hair should have made her happy. It was all rather confusing. But there'd been a moment in there—a vivid, *violent* moment—when she'd wanted to snatch the coffee out of his hands and throw it in his face.

It was perhaps just as well that her boss didn't emerge for the rest of the morning, or call her for more coffee to be delivered. Clearly, he was steeped in something important, some sudden programming brainwave or financial crisis which required his undivided attention.

In the month she'd been his PA, Rachel had discovered that Justin was a computer genius as well as a financial one, and had created several programs for following and predicting stock-market trends, as well as analysing other economical forces. Aside from her general secretarial duties, Rachel spent a couple of hours each day entering and downloading data into the extensive files these programs used. They needed constant updating to work properly.

She was completing that daily and slightly tedious area of her job shortly before noon, when the main door from the corridor opened and Justin's mother walked in.

Alice McCarthy was in her early sixties, a widow with two sons. She'd been one of Rachel's best customers during the four years she'd made ends meet by using her sewing skills at home. A tall, broad-shouldered woman with a battleship bust and surprisingly slender hips, Alice had difficulty finding clothing to fit off the peg. But she loved shopping for clothes, rather than having them made from scratch, and had more than enough money to indulge her passion. Mr McCarthy had been a very successful stockbroker in his day, and, according to Alice, a bit of a scrooge, whereas Alice veered towards the other extreme. Consequently, she was in constant need of a competent seamstress who could cleverly alter the dozens of outfits she bought each season.

Till recently that person had been Rachel, whom Alice had discovered when Rachel had distributed brochures advertising her sewing skills through all her local letterboxes. Alice lived only a couple of streets away from Lettie's house.

Despite the thirty-year age gap, the two women had got along well from the start. Alice's natural *joie de vivre* had brought some brightness into Rachel's dreary life. When her foster-mum passed away and her friends thought Rachel needed a job working outside of the home Alice had been generous enough to steer her into her present position, despite knowing this meant she had to find another person to alter her clothes. Fortunately, a salesgirl in one of the many boutiques Alice frequented had recommended an excellent alteration service in the city, run by two lovely Vietnamese ladies who were extremely efficient as well as inexpensive.

After Rachel had gone to work for her son Alice had

rung her at the office a couple of times to see how she was doing, but this was the first time she'd made a personal appearance.

'Alice!' Rachel greeted happily. 'What a lovely surprise. You're looking extremely well. Blue always looks good on you.'

Alice, who was as susceptible to a compliment as the next woman, beamed her pleasure. 'Flatterer. Nothing looks all that good on this unfortunate figure of mine. But I do my best. And my, aren't you looking a lot better these days? You've put on some weight. And you've changed your hair colour.'

Rachel's hand went up to pat the offending hair. 'Not for long. It goes back to brown tonight. I had it dyed for Isabel's wedding on Saturday. You remember Isabel, don't you? You met her at Lettie's funeral.'

'Yes, of course I remember her. Very blonde. Very beautiful.'

'That's the one. She wanted my hair red for the day. Of course, it wasn't done like this. It was down and curled. I also had more make-up on than a supermodel on a photo shoot.'

'I'll bet you looked gorgeous!'

'Hardly. But I looked OK for the occasion. And for the photographs. I'm well aware this colour red doesn't look any good on me normally.'

'But it might, you know, Rachel, if you wore some make-up. It's just that against your pale skin it looks too bright. And without any colour in your face that black suit you're wearing is too stark, by contrast. Now, if you were wearing blue,' she added, her own blue eyes sparkling, 'like the blue I've got on, and a spot of make-up, then that red hair just might be perfect.'

Rachel really wasn't in the mood for another woman to start trying to make her over. Isabel had been bad enough on the weekend. On top of that, she was still upset over Justin ignoring her this morning.

He wouldn't ignore her, however, if she started seriously tarting herself up. He'd think something was really up and then there would be hell to pay.

'Alice,' she said, slightly wearily. 'You were the one who told me about my predecessor, that flashy, flirtatious temp your son was so relieved to eject from his office. The reason Justin gave me this job is because he *likes* the way I look. He *likes* me *au naturel*.'

Alice rolled her eyes. In her opinion, no man liked women *au naturel*, even the ones who said they did. They all liked women to doll themselves up. You only had to watch men's eyes when a glamour-puss walked into a restaurant, or a party. Justin was simply going through a phase, a post-Mandy phase.

The trouble was, this phase was lasting far too long for her liking. It wasn't natural. Or healthy, either, for her son's mind or his body.

'That boy doesn't know *what* he likes any more,' she grumbled. 'That bitch of a wife of his certainly did a number on him. If ever I run into her again I'd like to…'

Whatever it was Alice was about to vow to do to her son's ex-wife was cut dead when the door to Justin's office was suddenly wrenched open, and the man of the moment appeared.

'Mum! I thought I heard a familiar voice. What are you doing here? And what were you talking about just then? Not gossiping about me to Rachel, were you?'

Alice's cheeks flushed but she managed not to look

too guilty. 'I never gossip,' she threw at her son defiantly. 'I only ever tell the truth.'

Justin laughed. 'In that case, why are you here? And no white lies, now. The truth, the whole truth and nothing but the truth.'

Alice shrugged. 'I came to the city early to do some shopping, didn't see a single thing I liked and decided on the spur of the moment to pop in and take you to lunch. Rachel too, if she'd like.'

'Oh, no, no, I can't,' Rachel immediately protested. 'I have some shopping that I simply have to do.' Namely, some brown hair dye.

'And neither can I,' Justin informed his mother. 'There was some unexpected bearish rumblings on the world stock markets last night and I have to have a report ready for the powers that be here before trading ceases today. So I'll be working through lunch. I was going to get Rachel to pop out and bring me back some sandwiches.'

'Poor Rachel,' Alice said. 'I thought the days of secretaries doing that kind of menial and demeaning job were over. I dare say you have her bring you coffee twenty times a day as well. I know how much you like your coffee. What else? Does she collect your dry-cleaning too?'

Justin looked taken aback. 'Well, yes, she has collected my dry-cleaning. Once or twice.' His eyes grew worried as they swung towards Rachel. 'Do you object to doing that kind of job, Rachel? You've never said as much.'

Rachel sighed. Of course she didn't object. If Alice thought those jobs were menial and demeaning, let her try changing urine-soaked sheets every morning.

'No, I don't mind at all. Really, Alice,' she insisted when Justin's mother looked sceptical. 'I don't.'

Now it was Alice's turn to sigh. 'No, you wouldn't. Just make sure you don't take advantage of Rachel's sweet nature,' Alice warned her son.

Rachel wished Alice would simply shut up.

Justin's eyes met hers again and she knew by their exasperated expression that he was thinking exactly the same thing. Rachel gave him a small smile of complicity, and his blue eyes twinkled back.

'I would never take advantage of Rachel,' he told his mother. 'I value her far too much to do anything to risk losing the best PA a man could have.'

Rachel's cheeks warmed at his flattering words.

She didn't realise at the time how ironic they were.

# CHAPTER THREE

MOST city singles loved Friday afternoons. Their moods would lift as the working week drew towards an end, anticipation building for that wonderfully carefree moment when they poured out of their office buildings and into their favourite bars and drinking holes for the traditional Friday-night drinks-after-work bash. Even the non-drinkers liked Fridays, because there was still the weekend to look forward to, two whole days without having to sit at their desks and their computers; two whole days of doing exactly as they pleased, even if that was nothing.

Rachel was one of the exceptions to the rule. Since coming back to work she hated the week to end because she hated the prospect of two whole days of doing just that. Nothing.

As she made her way to work the following Friday morning Rachel began thinking she might have to go shopping by herself this weekend after all, just for something to do. Last weekend had been OK, because of Isabel and Rafe's wedding. But this weekend was going to be dreadful, with Isabel away and that strangely soulless town house all to herself.

She could hardly fill the whole weekend with housework. She already kept the place spotless on a daily basis. She could read, of course, or watch television. But, somehow, indoor activities did not appeal. She felt like getting out and about.

It was a pity that the town house didn't have a garden. Unfortunately, the courtyard was all paved and the few plants dotted around were in pots. Rachel liked working with her hands. That was why she'd first taken up sewing as a teenager.

But sewing was on the no-no list for Rachel nowadays. She never wanted to see her sewing machine again. It was packed away at the back of a cupboard, never to see the light of day again. After the funeral, whenever she looked at it she thought of Lettie's illness, and all that had happened because of it. No nice associations at all.

Sometimes, she wished Justin would ask her to work overtime on the weekend. She knew he went into the office on a Saturday, so surely there was something she could do. Extra data entry, perhaps. Justin often had to farm some of that work out to an agency.

But he never asked, and she wouldn't dream of suggesting it. He might see her offer as evidence of a desire for more of his company, rather than the result of chronic loneliness.

Rachel glanced up at the sky before she entered her building. The clouds were heavier than the day before, the southerly change predicted earlier in the week having finally arrived yesterday, bringing intermittent showers.

The thought of more rain over the weekend dampened Rachel's enthusiasm for shopping by herself. Maybe she would wait till Isabel returned. There was no real hurry, now that Sydney's weather had changed back to cooler. Her black suits would do a while longer.

Yes, she decided as she swung through the revolving glass doors. Her shopping expedition could wait.

Justin was already in when she arrived. Surprisingly,

he'd put on the coffee machine and was in the act of pouring himself a mugful when she walked into the tea room. He was wearing one of her favourite suits, a light grey number which looked well against his dark hair and blue eyes, especially when teamed with a white shirt and blue tie.

'Morning,' he said, throwing her a warm smile over his shoulder. 'Want me to pour you one as well?'

'Yes, please,' she answered, her spirits lifting now that she was at work. She shoved her black bag and umbrella on the shelf under the kitchen-like counter, then took the milk out of the fridge, preferring her coffee white, though she could drink it black, at a pinch. Justin always had his black.

'What's it like outside?' he asked, and slid her mug along the counter to where she was standing.

'Overcast,' she said as she added her milk.

'Not actually raining, though?' he queried just before his mug made it to his lips.

'Not yet. But it will be soon.'

'Mmm.'

Rachel detected something in that 'mmm' which made her curious.

'Why?' she asked. 'Do you have something on this weekend which rain will spoil?'

He took the mug away from his mouth. 'Actually, no, just the opposite. I won't be here in Sydney at all. I'm flying up to the Gold Coast this afternoon to spend the weekend at a five-star ocean-front hotel.'

'Lucky you,' she replied, wondering who he was spending the weekend with.

'No need to feel jealous. You're coming with me.'

Rachel was grateful that she hadn't lifted her own

coffee off the counter, because she surely would have spilt it.

Justin chuckled. 'You should see the look on your face. But don't panic. I'm not asking you to go away with me for a dirty weekend. It's for work.'

Rachel closed her mouth then. Well, of course it was for work. How could she, even for a split-second, imagine anything else?

Silly Rachel.

'What kind of work?' she asked, finally feeling safe enough to lift her coffee off the counter and take a sip.

'A different kind of investment advice from my usual. Apparently, this holiday hotel—it's called Sunshine Gardens—is on the market and all potential buyers—of which AWI is one—are being flown up free of charge so they can see and experience first-hand the hotel's attractions and assets. Generally speaking we can do our own thing, except for tomorrow night, when we'll be wined and dined by management, after which there'll be a video shown, along with a presentation of facts and figures to con everyone into believing the hotel is a rock-solid investment. Guy Walters was supposed to go, but he can't, so he asked me to go in his place.'

Rachel frowned. 'Guy Walters. Who's he? I can't place him.'

'You must know Guy. Big, beefy fellow. Fortyish. Bald head. Exec in charge of property investments.'

Rachel searched her memory. 'No. No, I don't think I do. I'd remember someone who looked like that.'

Now Justin frowned. 'You're right. Guy hasn't been down here to see me personally since you started. Anyway, I do weights with him every morning. When I arrived this morning he wasn't there. He raced in half an hour later and explained that he was off to the airport to fly to Melbourne because his dad was ill, after which he explained about where he was supposed to be going and begged me to go in his place. Apparently, the CEO of AWI is super-keen on buying this place and is expecting a report on his desk first thing Monday morning, no excuses. Guy said I was the only one he could ask to go in his place whose opinion he would trust. He said he knew an old cynic like me wouldn't be blinded by surface appearances and would look for the pitfalls. At the same time, he also wanted a woman's opinion. He said women see things men don't always see.'

'So what woman was *he* going to take? His secretary? Or a colleague?'

'No, actually, he'd been going to take his wife. When I pointed out I didn't have a wife he said that shouldn't present a problem for a man-about-town like me, and I got all that male nudge-nudge, wink-wink crap. Guy's always implying I must have a little black book filled with the phone numbers of dozens of dolly-birds available for dirty weekends at a moment's notice.'

Rachel stopped sipping her coffee, her curiosity piqued. 'And you don't?'

'God, no.' The distaste on his face was evident. 'That's not my style.'

Rachel didn't know what to think. Maybe he simply didn't like women. Or maybe he just had old-fashioned principles and standards.

The thought that he might be right off sex—and women—was swiftly abandoned. The sceptic in Rachel couldn't see any heterosexual male of Justin's age and health being totally off sex no matter what. It went against everything she and all her female friends had come to believe about the human male animal.

'I told Guy I would be taking my valued and very astute PA,' Justin added. 'If you're available to go, of course. Are you?'

'Yes, but…'

'But what?'

'What about the accommodation? If this chap had been going with his wife, then…'

'I've already thought of that and there are no worries there. AWI's been allotted a two-bedroom apartment with two separate bathrooms, so there's no privacy issue. Also, you don't have to spend every minute of every day with me. You're free as a bird. I'd expect you to accompany me to the dinner on the Saturday night, however.'

'Er—what would I have to wear to something like that?'

'Guy said it's black tie. Lord knows why. Someone's being pretentious as usual. Probably their PR person. Do you have something suitable in your wardrobe? If not, I'm sure AWI can spare the expense of a dress. You could buy one up there tomorrow. Tourist towns usually have loads of boutiques.'

'No, I've got something suitable,' Rachel returned, thinking immediately of her bridesmaid dress, which Isabel had chosen specifically because it was the sort of dress you could wear afterwards. At the time, Rachel hadn't been able to imagine where, but it would be ideal for wearing to this dinner. As much as Justin might not like her coming into the office done up to the nines, surely he wouldn't want her to accompany him to a dinner looking totally colourless and drab.

A tiny thrill ran down her spine as she thought of

how surprised he might be if she wore her hair down and put on a bit of make-up. Nothing overdone, of course. A classy, elegant look.

'Great. And don't forget it's going to be a lot warmer up there at this time of year,' Justin went on. 'You'll need very light clothes for day wear. Very casual, too.'

Rachel saw the expression in his eyes as they flicked up and down the severely tailored black suit she was wearing.

'It's all right, Justin,' she said wryly. 'I do have some other more casual clothes.' Again, thanks to Isabel.

When Isabel's ex-fiancé broke off their engagement earlier this year Isabel had given Rachel her entire honeymoon wardrobe, bought to be worn on a tropical island. Rachel had thought at the time she would never have an opportunity to wear any of them, same as with the bridesmaid dress.

Now, suddenly, she did. What a strange twist of fate!

'So when is the flight?' she asked.

'It departs at four, which doesn't leave all that much time to do what has to be done here before we go. Unfortunately, I can't abandon my other work today entirely. I still need to check last night's markets and you'll still have to update the files. So, let's see, now…you live at Turramurra, don't you?'

'For the moment.'

He frowned. 'What do you mean, for the moment?'

'It's my friend's place. I've been staying with her temporarily since my foster-mum's funeral. Don't you remember? I told you all about Lettie and her illness at my interview.'

He slapped his forehead with the ball of his free hand and shot her an apologetic glance. 'Of course you did. You also said you'd be selling her old house and buying yourself a unit closer to the city. Sorry. I did listen to you that day. Honest. I'd just forgotten for the moment. So how's all that going? Found a buyer yet?'

Rachel sighed. 'Unfortunately, things haven't worked out the way I thought they would. Lettie did will me everything she owned, but it turned out she didn't own the house and contents in the first place. It was all still in her husband's name. I could have taken the matter to court but I just didn't have the heart. The solicitor said I probably wouldn't end up with much, anyway.'

'He's right there. Litigation is to be avoided at all costs. But gee, Rachel, that's a damned shame. And not fair, after all you did for your foster-mum. But then, life's not fair, is it?' he added with the bitterness of experience in his voice. 'So what are you going to do about a place to live?'

'Well, I'm house-sitting Isabel's town house whilst she's on her honeymoon. She won't be back for another fortnight. But I plan on renting a place of my own closer to the city after she does get back.'

'Flats near the city are expensive to rent,' Justin warned. 'Even the dumps.'

'Tell me about it. I've been looking in the paper. I can only afford a bedsit. Either that, or I'll have to share.' Which was a last resort. The idea of moving in with strangers did not appeal at all.

'Can't see you sharing a place with strangers,' Justin said, startling Rachel with his intuition. 'Can't you stay where you are in your friend's place? She won't be needing it, now that she's married.'

'She did offer it to me for a nominal rent.'

'Then take it and don't be silly,' he pronounced

pragmatically. 'So, how long do you think it would take you to go there, pack, then get back to the airport? I'll pay for taxis both ways, of course.'

'I don't think I could do it in less than two hours, and that's provided I don't hit any traffic snags. It is Friday, you know.'

'True. That means you'll have to leave here by one at the latest. Guy gave me the plane tickets, so I'll give you yours before you go and we'll meet at the allotted departing gate. OK?'

'Yes. OK.'

Justin smiled over the rim of his coffee mug. 'I knew I could count on you not to make a fuss. Any other woman would have had hysterics about how she'd need all day to get packed and changed, but not you.'

Rachel gave a rueful little laugh. 'I'm not sure if that's a compliment or a criticism.'

'A compliment,' Justin said drily. 'Trust me. Come on, let's get back to work. I want to have a clear desk and a clear head by the time that plane takes off this afternoon. I don't know about you, but I'm rather looking forward to having a break away from this office, not to mention this rotten weather. I've always been partial to some sun and surf. Which reminds me. Don't forget to pack a swimming costume. Even if you don't like the surf, the hotel has a great pool, I'm told.'

He plonked down his empty mug and marched off, leaving Rachel to stand there, staring after him, her stomach revolving as she recalled the bright yellow bikini amongst the clothes Isabel had given her.

The thought of swimming in a bright yellow bikini in front of her boss sent her into a spin.

'Hop to it, Rachel,' he threw over his shoulder.

She hopped to it, but she still kept thinking about

that bikini. Though modest by some standards, it was still a bikini. That, combined with the colour, would not present the non-flashy, non-flirtatious image Justin had of her and which he obviously felt comfortable with. She knew it was a stretch of the imagination that he would ever be sexually attracted to her—especially if he didn't like women—but in the end Rachel decided that the bikini would be accidentally left at home. She had a good thing going with her job and she didn't want to risk changing the status quo.

With this thought in mind, she decided not to wear her hair down for the dinner tomorrow night, either. It could go up as usual. And her make-up would be confined to a touch of lipstick. That was all she owned, anyway. It would be crazy to race out and buy a whole lot of stuff for one night. For what? Just to satisfy her feminine pride? Because that was all that was at stake. *Her* pride. Nothing to do with Justin. He obviously didn't give a damn how she looked.

Feeling much better with these decisions, Rachel put her mind to her job. At one o'clock on the dot she was off, the taxi making good time to Turramurra. Packing was a breeze. Isabel's discarded honeymoon gear was already in a very nice suitcase. It was just a matter of taking some things out, and adding some, namely her bridesmaid gear, along with her toilet bag. She did also add some white sandals from Isabel's wardrobe, knowing her friend wouldn't mind.

She didn't have time to change but she did put a simple white T-shirt on under her black jacket so that she could take the jacket off once they reached Coolangatta.

By two-ten she was back in a taxi, heading for Mascot, but this time the going was slower, because it had started to rain quite heavily. They fairly crawled down the Pacific highway. There was an accident at an intersection at Roseville, which caused a back-up, and they moved at a snail's pace again right down to Chatswood, after which the flow of traffic improved, courtesy of the new motorway. But her watch still showed five after three when she climbed out at the domestic terminal at Mascot. By the time she'd waited in line, been booked in and gone through Security, it was twenty-five to four, only ten minutes from the scheduled boarding time.

As she hurried along the long corridor towards the nominated gate Rachel hoped Justin wasn't worrying. She knew he'd already arrived because the lady on the check-in counter had been left instructions on her computer to give her the seat next to him.

Gate eleven came into sight at last, and so did Justin. He was sitting on a seat at the end of a row in the waiting area, reading an afternoon newspaper, and not looking at all anxious, though he did glance up over the top of the pages occasionally. When he spied her walking towards him he folded the newspaper, smiled and patted the spare seat beside him.

'You made it,' he said as she dropped down into it.

'Just. The traffic back into town was horrendous. I was wishing I had a mobile phone to call you and tell you my progress.'

'No worries,' he said. 'You're here now.'

'Yes. Yes. I'm here now.' Breathless, relieved and quite excited, now that she wasn't stressing about her clothes, or how she would look at tomorrow night's dinner. It had been years since she'd gone anywhere for the weekend and here she was, flying off to the Gold Coast in the company of a very attractive man.

OK, so he was only her boss, and there was nothing remotely romantic between them. But other people didn't know that. Other people might look at them and think that they *were* going off for a dirty weekend together.

*Not likely, you stupid girl,* a quite savage voice reprimanded inside her head. *Just look at him. He's gorgeous! The epitome of tall, dark and handsome. And just look at you. Talk about drabsville. A few years ago, things might have been different. You were a real looker then. Now you're a shadow of your former self. No, not even a shadow. A shell. That's what you are. A cold, empty, sexless shell!*

Rachel sagged back against the seat, a huge wave of depression swamping her earlier excitement.

'I think this trip'll do you good,' Justin said suddenly by her side.

'Oh?' she replied wearily. 'Why do you say that?'

'You've been a bit down-in-the-mouth since your friend's wedding last weekend. I dare say you're missing her. And it can't be much fun, working for a workaholic bore like me.'

She stared over at him. 'You're not a bore. I like my job. And I like working for you.'

He smiled at her. 'And I like you working for me. You are one seriously nice woman. Which is why what my mother said the other day has been bothering me. Tell it to me straight, Rachel. Do you object to bringing me coffee and running little errands for me? If you do, then I want you to say so. Right now.'

'Justin, I don't mind. Honestly. It's a change sometimes to get up and do something physical instead of just sitting at the computer, updating files.'

He frowned. 'That's a good portion of your job, isn't

it? Updating the files. That *must* be boring for someone of your intelligence. I should involve you more in what I do, explain my programs, show you how to analyse the data yourself, make proper use of that good brain of yours. Would you like that?'

'Oh! I…I'd *love* it! If—er—you really think I could do it, that is,' she added, her chronic lack of confidence not quite keeping up with her instant enthusiasm over his proposal.

'Of course you can. That way, when I set up my own company, I'll promote you to being a proper personal assistant with a salary to match, and we'll hire another girl to work on Reception and data entry.'

'Justin! I…I don't know what to say.'

'Just say yes, of course.'

She beamed at him. 'Yes, of course.'

'That's another thing I like about you. You don't argue with me. Aah, there's the boarding announcement. Come on, let's be one of the first on board. Then I can settle back to reading the newspaper and you can read that book you've got in your bag.' He was on his feet in a flash and off.

'How do you know I've got a book in my bag?' she asked after they'd been through the boarding-pass check and were striding down the tunnel towards the plane.

'Rachel, give me credit for *some* powers of observation,' he said drily. 'I do realise I have my nose buried in computer screens most of the day but I'd have to be a total moron not to notice some of your habits. You read every single lunch-hour. And I imagine every day on the train to and from work. Am I right?'

'Yes.'

'What kind of books do you like?'

'Oh. All kinds. Thrillers. Romances. Sagas. Biographies.'

'I used to read thrillers obsessively when I was at uni,' he said in a happily reminiscent tone. 'But I have to confess my reading rarely extends beyond the newspapers and business-based magazines these days.'

'I think that's a shame. Reading's a great pastime. And a good escape.'

'A good escape, eh? Yeah, you're right. It is. Maybe I should try it,' he muttered under his breath, 'instead of the gym.'

Rachel just caught this last possibly meant-for-his-ears-only remark, and wondered what he was trying to escape from. The memories of his marriage?

If his mother was to be believed then his ex-wife had been the bitch from hell. But if that was the case, then why would Justin have married her in the first place? He didn't strike Rachel as being a fool, or a pushover.

Relationships were a minefield, Rachel mused as she trailed after Justin past the welcoming flight attendants and into the body of the plane. And most marriages were a right mystery to all but the people involved. Justin's mother would naturally blame her son's wife for their break-up, but did she really know what had happened between the pair of them?

Justin stopped abruptly next to row D and turned to her. 'You have the window seat,' he said. 'I don't mind sitting on the aisle. Actually, it gives me a bit more leg room.'

'Thanks,' she said gratefully, and slid into the window seat. She liked to see where she was going.

Once settled, Rachel took out her book then stowed her black shoulder bag under the seat in front of her, ready for take-off. 'I hope it's not raining up there too,' she said as she peered out at the rain-soaked tarmac.

Justin looked up from the newspaper. 'It isn't according to the radar weather map I looked up on the internet just before I left the office. It's fine on the Gold Coast today with a top temperature of twenty-seven degrees. And more of the same is forecast for the weekend.'

'Sounds lovely,' she said with a happy sigh.

When Justin resumed reading his newspaper, Rachel opened the family saga she'd been reading the last couple of days. It wasn't riveting so far, but she liked the author and trusted her to get her in eventually.

Soon, she was off in that imaginative world of the story, so she didn't see the man who boarded the plane shortly afterwards. Or his female companion. If she had, Rachel would have recognised both of them.

She missed seeing them again at Coolangatta Airport, as it was so easy to do in crowds. Though, admittedly, she had been occupied chatting away with Justin at the luggage carousel and hadn't looked round at the other people waiting to collect their bags. She missed them again in the foyer of Sunshine Gardens, because she and Justin were already riding the lift up to their ocean-view apartment by the time they arrived.

Rachel might not have seen them at all till the following night at the dinner—which would have been an even greater disaster—if she hadn't discovered on reaching the door of their apartment that her door key didn't work.

'It must be faulty,' Justin said when his worked fine. 'I'll call the front desk when I get inside and they can bring you up another one.'

'No, I'll go back down now and get one myself,' Rachel said. 'You saw how busy they were.'

'Rachel, you're much too considerate sometimes.'

'Not really. I've always found it's quicker and less irritating to just do things myself, rather than wait for someone else to do it.'

'True. That's why I carried the luggage up myself instead of leaving it to the porter. I'm like you, I think. I can't stand waiting for things. When I want something I want it *now*. Off you go, then. I'll put your case in your bedroom and find the coffee-making equipment. Or would you rather I pour you a drink drink?'

'Coffee for now, I think. But you don't have to make it.'

'I know that. Call it repayment for services rendered.'

'Justin, you are much too considerate sometimes,' Rachel quipped as she hurried off, smiling when she heard his answering laugh.

Rachel had no sense of premonition as she rode the lift down to the ground-floor level again. Why should she have?

The lift doors opened and she walked out into the terracotta-tiled foyer, glancing around again at the décor as she made her way over to the reception desk.

Actually, this hotel reminded her of an island resort she'd gone to once with Eric. High ceilings, cool colours and glass walls overlooking lush green gardens with lots of water features.

Eric...

Now, there was a right selfish so-and-so if ever there was one. If she'd known how shallow he was she'd never have fallen in love with him in the first place, let alone agreed to marry him.

Rachel gave herself a swift mental shake. She wouldn't think about Eric. Ever again.

But, perversely, when she walked up to the reception desk the man booking in reminded her strongly of Eric, despite only viewing him from the back. He had the same sandy blond hair. The same way of holding his shoulders. The same elegance.

The attractive brunette standing next to him seemed familiar as well. Rachel listened to them chatting away together as they checked in, their voices horribly familiar.

And then, suddenly, they both turned around.

# CHAPTER FOUR

JUSTIN was suitably impressed the moment he stepped inside the apartment. It had a cool, comfy feel, with plenty of space, even to having its own foyer, which was unusual in hotel apartments.

As he dropped their two suitcases next to the hall stand—a sturdy yet elegant piece with a smoked-glass top and carved oak base—Justin caught a glimpse of himself in the matching mirror above. His hair, which possibly needed a cut, was all over the place. That's what happened when you had to walk across windy tarmac, as they had at Coolangatta airport. No tunnels to spoil you.

Straightening, Justin smoothed back the wayward top and sides with the flat of his hands, then moved a little closer to the mirror to peer at the bags under his eyes.

Could do with a good eight hours' sleep, he thought as he turned and went over to slot his room key into the gizmo beside the door. The lights came on automatically, as did the air-conditioning. That done, Justin strode into the main living area, where he stripped off his jacket and tie, tossed them over the back of one of the nearby dining chairs then took himself on a quick tour of the rest of the apartment.

Absolutely everything met with his approval, even the crisp citrus colours they'd used on the walls and soft furnishings. Normally, lime and yellow and orange would not be to his taste but the brightness was offset by the wall-to-wall cream carpet, the cream woodwork and the extensive use of pine. The kitchen was all pine, with white counter-tops and white appliances, and the bathrooms—thank heaven—were white as well. Justin had had about enough of that all-over black marble in the hideously pretentious bathroom at his office.

He contemplated giving Rachel the main bedroom, then decided she would only protest, so he put her bag in the second bedroom, which suffered little for size. Both bedrooms also had access to the balcony that stretched the full length of the apartment and had a view that looked pretty spectacular, even from inside.

How much better would it look from the balcony itself?

Justin decided to find out before making the coffee, and wasn't disappointed. You could see for miles, from Tweed Heads on his right to Surfer's Paradise in the northern distance with its tell-tale skyline of skyscrapers. The sea was looking breathtakingly beautiful, even now, with the sun having set and the sky darkening from its earlier bright blue to a dusky grey. Admittedly, first thing in the morning the sun might be a bit too brilliant as it rose over the horizon and slammed straight into the windows behind him, but in the afternoon and evenings it would be wonderful to sit outside here in one of the deckchairs, sipping some chilled white wine.

'I wonder if Rachel likes white wine,' he said to himself, and seriously hoped so, because the scenario he'd just pictured in his mind didn't seem quite so appealing on his own. He would ask her when she got back, and if she did he'd see about having Room Service send up a bottle or two. Then later he'd take her to the swankiest restaurant in the place for dinner.

Hotels like this always had at least one à la carte eating establishment.

Rachel deserved a bit of spoiling, he decided, after all she'd been through these past few years.

Justin breathed in the refreshing salt-sea air for thirty seconds longer before returning to the living area and going in search of the coffee-making equipment. It crossed his mind whilst he rummaged around in the cupboards that Rachel was taking a good while. Presumably, the front desk was still busy. Or maybe they couldn't find another key to this room. He made a mental note to find out what had actually happened. Guy would want to know what he thought of the service. The last thing a new owner needed to do was to have to sack staff then find replacements. Far too expensive and time-consuming an operation.

The electric jug found, Justin filled it and put it on, then set about emptying a small packet of—wow!—*quality* coffee into each of the two white mugs he'd located. No cheap muck. That was good. Very good. He hated hotels that supplied low-grade products. He'd have to remember to ask Rachel what the shampoo and conditioner were like. He could actually never tell the good from the bad in that department, but a woman would know. Guy was right in that regard.

The water had boiled and Justin was standing there, deciding whether to pour his or wait for Rachel to come back, when there came a knock on the door. He hurried over to answer it, tut-tutting to himself on the way.

'You don't have to tell me,' he said when he wrenched open the door to find Rachel on the other side. 'They didn't have another key.'

Rachel just stood there, her face ashen, her eyes anguished, her hands clutched tightly in front of her.

Justin, despite not being the most intuitive male in the world, was quick to appreciate her distressed state.

'Rachel!' he exclaimed. 'What is it? What's happened?'

'I…I…'

Clearly, she could not go on, her throat making convulsing movements as she struggled for control.

'Come inside,' Justin said and, taking her left elbow, steered her quite forcibly into the apartment. Her hands remained clutched tightly in front of her and she looked as if she was going to burst into tears, or faint.

Once Justin had kicked the door shut behind them, he guided her over to the three-seater opposite the television and plonked her down into the middle cushion, then sat on the pine coffee-table, facing her.

'Rachel,' he said softly, taking her still clasped hands within his. 'Tell me what happened?'

She gave a small laugh that held a decided edge of hysteria.

'What happened?' she repeated. 'They didn't recognise me, that's what happened. *He* didn't recognise me. Can you believe that?'

'Who's he?'

'Eric.'

'Who's Eric?'

'My fiancé,' she choked out, 'till I told him I was leaving my job to stay home and mind Lettie.' She started shaking her head as though still not quite believing the situation she found herself in. 'I thought I knew why he broke our engagement,' she went on in shaken tones. 'I thought he didn't love me enough, or care enough to support my decision. It never crossed my mind that there might have been another woman in the wings all along, and that I'd given him the perfect excuse to call our wedding off.'

'What makes you think there was another woman at the time?'

'Because I've just seen the bitch,' she said, surprising Justin with the unexpected flash of venom. 'She was downstairs just now, checking in with him.'

'And she is…?' Justin probed, knowing it couldn't be Rachel's best friend, since she was overseas on her honeymoon. Thank God.

'The real-estate agent who sold him the fancy unit which was supposed to be our marital home,' she elaborated bitterly.

'I see. And are *they* married now?'

'No. Living together, I presume from the conversation I overheard at the desk. Either that or they just go away together on what he called weekend junkets associated with her job.'

'I see,' Justin said again, trying to think of something to say to pacify her. But he knew how hard that was, when your emotions were involved. 'Look, you don't really know he was carrying on with this woman before he left you, Rachel. You're just jumping to conclusions.'

'No, I'm not. I know I'm right. I had a feeling about them at the time but I ignored it. I told myself that I was imagining the intimate little looks which used to pass between them, and the many excuses he made to meet up with her at the unit when I was busy at work. Eric's a top lawyer, you see, and can pretty well come and go as he pleases.'

'OK. So he's a two-timing rat as well as a shmuck.

What does it matter now? You can't possibly still be in love with him. Not after…how long ago was it?'

'Four years, give or take a month.'

'See? Now, if you'd said a year maybe, or eighteen months…' like in his case with Mandy '…then I'd understand why you're so upset.'

'Love doesn't stop simply because you want it to, Justin. Even if I didn't love Eric any more, I wouldn't be human if I didn't hate seeing him with another woman like that. But I'm doubly upset because neither of them *recognised* me!' she finished on a strangled sob.

Sympathy *and* empathy consumed Justin as he realised what she was saying. Her hurt was not solely because of this Eric's former betrayal, but because he hadn't recognised her physically.

Justin understood that type of humiliation well and his heart went out to her.

'Maybe he wasn't really looking at you,' he tried excusing. 'Maybe he was off in another world.'

'I wish. But no. He bumped into me when he turned away from the check-in desk. Almost knocked me over. He actually grabbed my shoulders and looked right at me for a second or two. He saw me well enough and there was not a hint of recognition. *She* didn't recognise me, either. Though I can't really blame her. She didn't know me all that well. We only met a couple of times. And I know I've changed a lot. But Eric should still have known me. We were lovers, for pity's sake!'

'Did you say something to him? Call him by name?'

'*Speak* to him? No.' She shuddered. 'I bolted into the ladies' room in the foyer and stayed there till I was sure they'd have left the area and gone up to whatever floor they're staying on. That's what took me so long.'

What probably took her so long, Justin believed, was the time she'd spent in there, weeping and looking in the mirror to see what it was this Eric had seen, and *not* seen.

'Do you think he…um…might have been pretending not to know you?'

'No. There was nothing like that in his eyes. Just blankness. He didn't recognise me.'

'Have you changed *that* much in four years, Rachel?'

Her shoulders sagged, her eyes clouding to an expression of utter misery. 'I guess I must have.'

'So what do you want to do?' he asked, his own spirits sagging at the realisation that this weekend wasn't going to be such a happy or relaxing getaway after all.

'About what?' she asked wearily.

'Presumably this couple will be at the dinner tomorrow night. That must be the junket you heard mentioned.'

Horror filled her face at the prospect.

'You don't have to go,' he said quickly.

'Are you sure? I mean…I don't like to let you down but I…I don't think I could bear it. Eric might recognise me after I do myself up a bit. But, there again, he might not. Either way, I'm going to be terribly uptight, and very poor company with few powers of observation.'

'It's all right, Rachel. Truly. I'll go by myself.' He let her hands go and straightened.

She stared up at him, and he realised her hazel eyes were really quite lovely. How could that fool have not recognised her, if he'd been her lover? Eyes were the one thing which never changed. How many times would this Eric have stared down into Rachel's eyes when they'd been in bed together?

Hell, Mandy's beautiful blue eyes were imprinted on his brain!

His sigh carried a wealth of emotions of his own. 'I'll go finish making us that coffee.' And he stood up.

'You are such a nice man,' she choked out, then burst into tears, burying her face in her hands.

Smothering a groan, Justin sat himself down next to her and took her into his arms, cradling her weeping face against his shirt front.

'No decent human being,' he said gently as he stroked her back, 'could be anything but nice to you, Rachel. This Eric is scum. You're better off without him.'

'I know that,' she sobbed. 'But it still hurts to see him with another woman.'

'I'm sure it does,' Justin murmured soothingly. God knows how *he'd* react if he ever ran into Mandy with that swine who'd stolen her away from him, he thought. Murder was too good for the pair of them.

'Maybe seeing him again like that is a good thing,' he tried, though not quite believing it himself. 'It should give you the motivation to forget him once and for all and get on with your own life. After all, life isn't too bad for you now, is it? You have a job you like, with a considerate boss. Or so you said,' he added wryly. 'And soon you'll have an even better job with enough of a wage coming in to afford a seriously nice place to live in of your own. What more could you possibly want?'

'To still be beautiful,' she mumbled into his chest.

Justin reached down and took her hands away from where they were jammed under her chin, then tipped her face up so that their eyes met. 'You *are* still beautiful, Rachel,' he said softly. 'Where it counts.'

'Right,' she said ruefully. 'Pardon me if I don't get too excited by that compliment. I've found that beauty on the inside is highly overrated as an asset, especially when it comes to the opposite sex.'

'Not all men are as shallow as your Eric,' he countered, confident that he didn't judge a woman so superficially.

'Is that so? Might I ask you a rather personal question?'

'Shoot.'

'Was your ex-wife beautiful?'

Justin opened his mouth, then closed it again. Mandy had been drop-dead gorgeous, there was no doubt about it. She had a very pretty face, big blue eyes, long blonde hair. A *great* figure. And she'd known how to showcase herself to perfection, from the top of her glossy blonde head to the tips of her pink-painted toes.

Rachel, on the other hand, was a far cry from drop-dead anything. Yet she wasn't ugly. She couldn't even be called plain. Aside from having genuinely lovely eyes, she had regular features in her oval-shaped face and an interesting mouth, now that he bothered to really look. Wide, and tilted up at the corners, with a very full bottom lip.

It was just that she always looked so colourless, like a picture that had faded badly. The black suits she wore to work looked extra-drab on her, as did the clunky mid-heeled black shoes.

As for her hair...

He could not think of a good thing to say about her

hair, except that it was far better not red, as it had been last Monday, because any attention brought to it could only create a more negative impression.

'Case closed,' Rachel said succinctly, and stood up. 'God, I feel terrible. I must look terrible too. I think I'll go and have a shower and change. Which way to my room?'

'What about coffee?'

'Thank you but I don't feel like it just now.'

Me neither, he thought. He needed something much more potent in the drinks department. Some food was in order as well. Time was getting on and he hadn't had anything to eat since breakfast except that on-board snack. He wouldn't mind betting Rachel hadn't had any lunch either. No wonder she was so thin.

Though not *that* thin, he'd realised when he was holding her close just now. She had some reasonable breasts hiding there underneath that black jacket. Either that, or she'd been wearing a padded bra.

'Showering and changing sounds like a good idea,' he agreed, determined not to spend all weekend wearing a suit. Bad enough he had to tog up in a tux tomorrow night. 'Your room's on the right down that hallway. The bathroom's opposite on the left. I left your case at the foot of the bed. I'm going to pop into the shower too, but first I'll order us something to eat from Room Service, since going out to dinner tonight is out of the question now. You wouldn't want to run into yours truly and his lady-love. And no, please don't say again what a nice man I am.'

She gave him a faint smile. 'All right.'

'Go, go, go.' He waved her off.

Once Rachel went, he crossed to the desk, which held the leather-bound folder that listed all the hotel's services, plus the in-house menu. He ran his eye swiftly down and decided on something cold. A platter of mixed seafood and a couple of different salads, followed by strawberries and cream, all washed down with a bottle of their best white wine.

Most women liked white wine and Rachel needed cheering up.

Frankly, so did he.

He always did after thinking about Mandy.

Room Service arrived half an hour later, with Justin able to answer the door totally refreshed and dressed in beige cargo shorts and a dark red polo shirt. His feet he'd happily left bare for now. With the food safely deposited in the fridge, and the waiter tipped and dispensed with, Justin set about opening the bottle of wine, a Chablis, after which he popped it in the portable wine cooler provided.

The wine glasses supplied weren't exactly top-drawer crystal but they were nice enough. He placed two of them in the fridge to chill then wandered down the hallway to see how Rachel was progressing. He'd heard her shower going for ages earlier on.

'You ready yet, Rachel?' he asked, stopping in the hall between both shut doors, her bedroom and the bathroom. He didn't know which room she was in.

'Not really.' Her voice came from the bedroom.

'What do you mean, not really?'

'I have a slight problem.'

'What's that?'

'I—er—washed my smalls in the shower before I realised I'd forgotten to pack any more.'

Justin had to struggle not to laugh. But Rachel without underwear was so *un*-Rachel. 'That's OK. Just put

on a robe for now. They'll dry by morning, then you
can go shopping for more.'

'Er…'

'Don't tell me you didn't pack a robe, either.'

'No, no, I do have a robe but it's a bit…um…'

'What?'

'Nothing. I suppose I'm silly to worry,' she muttered.

'Put it on, then, and get yourself out here. Your pre-
dinner drink awaits.'

'OK. I…I'll just be a minute.'

'I'll be out on the balcony, waiting. Don't be too
long. I hate drinking alone.'

Justin was lounging back in a deckchair, sipping his
wine and thinking life wasn't too bad after all, when
he heard the glass door slide back from down Rachel's
end. His head turned just in time to see her step out
onto the balcony.

Justin did his best not to do a double take, or to stare.
But, hell, it was hard not to.

The robe Rachel was wearing was not a modest little
housecoat by any means, but a very sexy emerald-green
satin number which clung as only satin could.
Admittedly it had sleeves to the elbow and did reach
down to her ankles. And she *had* sashed it tightly, but
this only seemed to emphasise the surprisingly shapely
and obviously naked body underneath it.

Clearly, she hadn't been wearing a padded bra earlier, Justin realised as his gaze took in the natural full-
ness of her breasts, which were very nice indeed.
Actually, her body was very nice all round. She had a
deliciously tiny waist and enough curve to her hips to
look very feminine and, yes, almost sexy.

Amazing what had been hiding underneath those awful black suits she'd been wearing to the office!

Amazing what that awful hairdo had been hiding as well. Having her hair down and curling damply onto her shoulders took years off her face. There was some much-needed colour in her complexion as well, possibly from the heat of the shower, which gave him a glimpse of what she might look like with some make-up on.

Maybe still not a beauty queen but one hell of a lot better than her usual colourless façade. With the right kind of dress she could look quite fabulous. That figure of hers was a knock-out.

When she started coming towards him the robe flapped back at the knees, revealing a full length matching nightie underneath, which was perhaps just as well. He didn't want to stare too much or she was sure to get embarrassed. Even so, it was a very sexy outfit and not the sort of lingerie Justin would have expected Rachel to own, let alone wear.

Still, seeing her in it gave him an idea which just might salve some of Rachel's pride and give him some personal satisfaction as well. He already hated this Eric creep for what he'd done to such a nice woman. Dumping her was bad enough, but fancy not recognising her!

Of course, Rachel was her own worst enemy when it came to her appearance. Obviously, she could look a whole lot better than she did every day.

If she'd do what he was going to suggest, however, then, come tomorrow night, dear old Eric was bound to recognise her. And Rachel would never have to scuttle off and hide in a ladies' room again, weeping with hurt and humiliation. She'd be able to hold her head high in any company and show her pathetic ex-fiancé that he'd made a big mistake in dumping her.

A *big* mistake.

*Just as Mandy made a big mistake dumping you?* came the dark and caustic thought. *Is it vengeance for Rachel you want here, or some vengeance for yourself?*

Mandy, he thought angrily. Always, it came back to Mandy!

# CHAPTER FIVE

WHEN Rachel saw Justin's sudden scowl she stopped walking towards him. She hadn't minded his surprise on first seeing her dressed as she was. Surprise was fair enough. But a scowl was another matter entirely.

'I...I think I'd better go back and find something else to put on,' she said. 'This just isn't appropriate, is it?'

'Certainly not!' he exclaimed, then astonished her by laughing. 'No, no, that's not what I meant. I meant don't go back inside and change. You look perfectly fine as you are. Heavens, Rachel, you're wearing more clothes than most girls wear walking down the street up here. Here, sit down and get some of this wine into you.' He swept up a bottle of white wine from the portable cooler standing by his chair and poured her a glass.

'I hope you like Chablis,' he said as he placed the glass on the white outdoor table and pushed it across to where she was settling herself in one of the matching white chairs.

'Yes, I do. Thank you.' Rachel was grateful for the drink, but more grateful to be sitting down, and no longer on show. That short walk along the balcony had felt like a million miles. Talk about embarrassing!

The whole situation was embarrassing. Fancy forgetting to bring any underwear.

She picked up the wine glass, cradled it in both her

hands to stop them shaking and took a sip. 'Oh, yes,' she sighed. 'This *is* good.'

'It ought to be,' Justin said with a smile in his voice. 'It cost a small fortune. But no sweat. Everything's on the house, according to Guy. I aim to take full advantage of it. And so should you. Which gives me an idea. Wait here.'

He put down his wine and levered himself up from the chair. 'Won't be long,' he said, and hurried back inside through the sliding glass doors, leaving Rachel to do a spot of staring of her own.

It was strange seeing her boss in a bright top, casual shorts and bare feet. She'd always known he sported a nice shape and tan, but she'd never seen so much of it before. Even his bare feet were brown, which made her wonder what a man who wore shoes and socks all week did to achieve that. Lie in one of those sunbeds at the gym? Or swim a lot in an outdoor pool? If so, where? She knew he lived in a high-rise apartment in an exclusive complex down on the harbour foreshore at Kirribilli, so it probably sported a pool. Exclusive ones usually did.

'I thought as much,' Justin was saying as he returned through the open glass doors, carrying an open black leather folder. 'They do have a beauty salon in this place.'

'A…a beauty salon?' Rachel repeated, not sure what Justin was getting at.

'Yes. Seeing you wearing that gorgeous green and with your hair down has shown me, Rachel Witherspoon, that you have been hiding your light under a bushel. I don't know if anyone has ever told you before but black does nothing for you, and neither does the way you wear your hair to work. You also have a damned good figure, which your working wardrobe doesn't show to advantage. With a different hairstyle, some make-up and the right clothes, Rachel, you could look more than good. You could look great.'

'But…'

'But what?'

'But I thought you didn't want me looking great, especially at work.'

'What?'

'Your mother told me all about your previous PA long before you ever did.'

He grimaced. 'Oh, God, she didn't, did she?'

'Afraid so.'

He frowned over at her. 'So you *deliberately* made yourself look like a plain Jane to get the job.'

Not really, an amazed Rachel was thinking. She'd just come *au naturel*. She *was* a plain Jane. But she wasn't about to say so. She rather liked the thought that Justin believed she'd been down-playing a whole host of hidden attractions.

'Well…' she hedged, not sure what to say at this juncture.

'Oh, Rachel, Rachel, you didn't have to do that. I'd have given you the job, anyway, because I saw right from the start that you were nothing like that other girl. It wasn't just the way she dressed, you know, but the way she acted. Like some oversexed vamp all the time. She drove me insane.'

'So you wouldn't mind if I did myself up a bit for work?'

'Why should I mind?'

'I was worried that if I suddenly came into the office with a new hairdo and a new wardrobe you might think I was…um…'

'Tarting yourself up for me?'

'Yes,' she said sheepishly.

He laughed. 'I would never think that of you. Silly Rachel.'

Rachel tried not to be offended. But she was, all the same. Yes, silly, *silly* Rachel.

'Which brings me right back to my original suggestion,' he went on. 'Now, tomorrow I want you to go down to that beauty salon and get the works. Facial, massage, pedicure, manicure, waxing, hair, make-up. The lot. It says here they do all that.'

'That seems excessive.' Even for me, she thought ruefully.

'No, it's not. It's necessary.'

'Oh, thank you very much,' came the waspish comment.

'Now, now, this is no time for over-sensitivity, Rachel. The truth is you've let yourself get into bad habits with this plain-Jane nonsense. I can understand that you might not have bothered with your appearance much when you were at home all the time, but I'll bet there was a time when you went to a lot of trouble with your hair and make-up and clothes.'

'We-ll…'

'*Well?*' he probed forcefully.

'I always suspected I didn't become a finalist in the Secretary of the Year competition on my office skills alone,' she said drily.

'I don't doubt it. I'll bet you were a looker back then.'

'I was…attractive.'

'And you never wore black.'

'Not often.'

'How did you wear your hair?'

'Down,' she admitted. 'With auburn highlights.'

'No wonder people from your past didn't recognise you today. But, come tomorrow night, Eric the Mongrel will recognise you all right.'

'Eric the Mongrel?' she repeated on a gasp.

'Yeah. That's what I've nicknamed him. Do you like it?'

'Oh, dear. I *love* it.'

'So you'll do it? Come to the dinner with me?'

Rachel swallowed. It would take every bit of courage she owned to face Eric and that woman once more, even if she was dolled up to the nines. But, by God, she would!

'Yes,' she said, and Justin beamed.

'Fantastic. Here. A toast is in order.'

He held his glass out towards her and she clicked it with hers.

'To the comeuppance of Eric the Mongrel,' Justin pronounced.

Rachel's stomach flipped over. 'Comeuppance?'

'Oh, yes. Your ex deserves a few serves. And I'm just the man to deliver them!'

Justin paced up and down the living room, impatient for Rachel to make her appearance. She'd stayed hidden ever since her return from the beauty salon around five, letting herself in whilst he'd been in the bathroom, shaving. Now it was getting on for seven and he was dressed in his tux and ready to go down for the cocktail party that preceded the dinner at eight, an arrangement Rachel was well acquainted with. They'd discussed it last night.

So when seven came and went without her showing,

Justin strode down the hallway and knocked firmly on
her door.

'Enough titivating in there, Rachel. It's seven
o'clock. Time you faced the music.'

'Coming,' she called back. But nervously, he
thought.

The door opened and Justin's blue eyes rounded.

'Wow, Rachel. You don't just look great. You look
fabulous!'

Even that was an understatement. Where had his
plain-Jane PA disappeared to? In her place stood a
striking creature. No, a stunning creature. No, a striking, stunning, *sexy* creature.

Justin found himself standing there, just staring at
her, trying to work out what she'd done to cause such
a dramatic transformation.

It couldn't just be her hair, though it was very different. And very red, he noted wryly. Cut in layers, it
fell from an off-centre parting to her shoulders, framing
her face and her *eyes*, her always lovely eyes, which
now looked not just lovelier but larger. Was it the
smoky eye make-up which had achieved this effect, or
some other subtle change? Whatever, when he looked
into her face he couldn't stop looking at her eyes.

They looked back at him, heartbreakingly hesitant.
She still didn't know how beautiful she was. How
amazingly, incredibly beautiful.

'You honestly think so?' she asked. 'You don't think
I look...foolish?'

'Foolish?' he echoed in disbelief. 'In what way could
you possibly look foolish?'

'My hair colour bothers me for starters. It's too red,'
she said, touching it gingerly with her equally red nails.

'Honey, you can carry off red now,' he reassured softly.

'Oh...' She blushed prettily. 'But don't you think the make-up girl put too much foundation on me? I look like a ghost.'

'No, you don't. That's the fashion. You know, that's the slinkiest bridesmaid dress I think I've ever seen,' he remarked, shaking his head as his gaze ran down the dress again.

It was a turquoise silk sheath, with thin shoulder straps and a fitted waist that showed off Rachel's nice bustline and tiny waist to perfection. The skirt was straight and slender, and fell to mid-calf, with a slanted hem from which hung strands of crystal beads. Under this rather provocative feature her legs were bare, yet looked as smooth and shiny as they would if covered in the most expensive stockings. Her feet were shod in turquoise high heels, which matched the colour of the dress and had open toes, showing scarlet-painted toes. She smelled faintly of jasmine, possibly from a scented oil used to massage her skin. Her arms, Justin also noted as his eyes travelled back up to her face, looked as soft and shiny as her legs, probably the result of a full body massage today.

That beauty salon deserved a medal for the miracle it had managed in one short day. Not that he'd tell Rachel that. Despite her fab new look, her self-esteem was still wavering, which was a problem. Frankly, he'd been looking forward to exacting some well-deserved revenge on rotten exes tonight, and he needed Rachel's full co-operation to achieve that end. Clearly, her confidence still needed some more boosting.

'You look good enough to eat, Rachel. Eric the

Mongrel is going to be jealous as sin when I walk into that dinner party with you on my arm.'

'I think it's Eric's girlfriend who might be the jealous one,' Rachel returned as she looked him up and down.

Justin was surprised but pleased that she thought him attractive. It would make his plan for the evening run smoother. 'Yes, we've both cleaned up rather well, haven't we? Come on, let's go and put a cat amongst the pigeons. Do you have a bag?'

'No, I don't.'

'No need. It's not as though we have to go outside. There'll be no wind to mess up your hair. If you feel in the need for any repairs during the night you can always whip up here in the lift. I'll have my key card with me.'

'Yes, I might need to do that after dinner. I always eat off my lipstick, though the make-up girl who did me up said this particular brand is renowned for not coming off. She said it's the one the actresses use who make blue movies.'

Justin laughed and started shepherding Rachel towards the door. 'That's handy to know. So if you disappear under the tablecloth at any time tonight I'll feel confident you'll resurface still looking immaculate.'

When she looked scandalised Justin tut-tutted. 'Come, now, Rachel, try to get with the spirit of this occasion. Remember, I'm not just your boss for tonight. I'm your lover as well.'

*'What?'* She ground to a startled halt.

Justin was taken aback. 'I thought you understood that was part of my plan. Look, how else are we going to get up Eric the Mongrel's nose, unless he thinks we're a hot item? We want him to believe you haven't missed him one bit, that you've survived his callous dumping; you did your duty to Lettie like the angel you are and are now moving on to a much more exciting and fulfilling life than you would have had married to him. You're looking better than ever. You live in a fantastic town house at Turramurra. And you have this great new job, with a handsome, successful, besotted boss who can't keep his hands off you.'

'But…but I wouldn't *like* having a boss like that!'

'You might not, but it's some men's fantasy. And some women's. Trust me on that. I would imagine it was right up Eric the Mongrel's alley.'

'You have to stop calling him that or I'm going to giggle all night.'

'That's all right. Giggling's good.'

'But it's not *me*.'

'It can be. You can be anything you want to be tonight. The point of this exercise is to show your ex that he doesn't know you at all, if he ever did. And to make him want the new you like crazy!'

'I…I don't think…'

'Now, thinking's a definite no-no for this evening as well. Thinking rarely does anyone any good. Just follow my lead, honey, and everything will be fine.'

When he took her elbow he felt her resistance and stared down at her. She stared back up at him.

'You called me honey.'

'Well, I'm not going to call you Rachel all the time. Sounds far too platonic. OK, so honey's out. How about the occasional darling? Yes, that's much better. Much classier. Come along, Cinders, darling,' Justin said with a rueful smile. 'It's time to go to the ball.'

# CHAPTER SIX

RACHEL stood silently by Justin's side in the ride down in the lift, her stomach twisted into nervous knots.

How could she possibly carry this charade off? It was...beyond her. She might be looking good on the outside but inside she was still the same Rachel who'd run into Eric yesterday and bolted like a frightened horse. Fear rippled down her spine and invaded every pore in her body. The thought of confronting her ex with his new lady-love held nothing but a sick-making apprehension.

'I...I can't do this, Justin,' she whispered just as the lift stopped at one of the floors on the way down to the lobby.

'Yes, you can,' he reassured firmly.

The lift doors whooshed back and there, waiting for the lift, were the objects of her fear.

Rachel sucked in sharply.

'I gather that's Eric the Mongrel,' Justin whispered.

'Yes,' she choked out, not feeling at all like giggling at the silly nickname this time. Eric the Magnificent would be more like it. He really was a drop-dead gorgeous-looking guy, especially in a dinner suit. Charlotte was no slouch in the looks department, either, the passing years seeming to have enhanced her darkly striking beauty. Tall and supermodel-slim, she was chic personified with her concave-cut dark brown bob and elegant black dress.

'Charlotte, come on,' Eric said impatiently, stepping

forward to hold the lift doors open whilst not giving its occupants a second glance.

Charlotte, who'd been checking her hair and make-up in the hall mirror when the lift doors opened, finally swung round. 'Keep your shirt on, lover,' she said. 'These things never start on time.'

As Charlotte walked past Eric into the lift he glanced up over her shoulder and finally noticed Rachel in the corner, his face registering instant recognition this time, plus considerable shock.

'Good lord!' he exclaimed. 'It's Rachel. You remember Rachel, Charlotte. Rachel Witherspoon.'

Rachel would later wonder where her courage—and her composure—came from. Possibly from the look of surprise on that bitch's face as she surveyed Rachel from top to toe.

'So it is,' Charlotte said. 'Fancy seeing you here, of all people.' Her sexily slanting black eyes soon slid over to Justin. Women like Charlotte never looked at other women for long when there were attractive men around.

Meanwhile, Eric kept staring at *her* as though she were a little green man from Mars.

'I was just thinking the same about you two,' Rachel returned, proud as punch of her cool control. 'I gather you're together? This is my boss, Justin McCarthy,' she swept on, not giving either of them the chance to answer. 'Justin, these are friends of mine, Eric Farmer and Charlotte—er—sorry. I can't seem to recall your second name, Charlotte.'

'Raper.'

'Oh, yes. Raper…' A ghastly surname. 'So what brings you two up to the Gold Coast this weekend? Business, or pleasure?'

Eric muttered 'Pleasure' the same time as Charlotte said 'Business'. After Charlotte shot him an angry look he changed his answer to 'Both'. But he looked far from happy.

Rachel had to smile at having rattled Eric so easily. Justin was right. A spot of revenge was a good salve for old wounds. But she still wasn't sure about pretending she and Justin were lovers.

'And you?' Eric finally thought to ask. 'Are you here for business or pleasure?' He too was assessing Justin on the quiet, Rachel noticed. And perhaps not feeling his usual male superiority. For, as glamorous as Eric still looked at first glance, up close there was some evidence he was beginning to go to seed. He was becoming jowly, his crowning glory was thinning on top and his stomach was no longer athletically flat.

Frankly, he was looking a bit flabby. Of course, he had to be going on forty nowadays, whereas Justin was in his earlier thirties. Justin was taller than Eric, too. Taller and fitter and possibly more attractive, Rachel was surprised to discover.

'We're just here on business, aren't we, Justin?' she said, and touched him lightly on his nearest arm, her eyes pleading with him not to say differently.

Justin covered her hand with his and gave it an intimate little squeeze. 'Oh, absolutely,' he agreed, whilst his glittering blue eyes gave an entirely different message. 'Rachel's my new PA, and such a treasure. Only been with me for five weeks or so, but I already wouldn't know what I'd do without her.'

Oh, God, Rachel agonised. Somehow, without saying a word to that effect, Justin was making it sound as though their relationship extended way beyond the office.

'Really,' Eric said coldly, one eyebrow arching as he stared at her cleavage.

Rachel could feel heat gathering in her cheeks because it was perfectly clear what Eric was thinking.

'Eric,' Charlotte said sharply. 'Will you please move your butt inside the lift so that the doors can close?'

He flashed his lover a caustic glance but took a step inside.

'Have you known Rachel long?' Justin asked him whilst they waited for the lift to resume its ride down.

Rachel immediately tensed over what answer he would give.

'We were engaged once a few years back,' Eric bit out. 'But things didn't work out at the time, did they, Rach?'

Everything inside Rachel tightened further at his use of that once affectionate shortening of her name. But she'd be damned if she'd show any reaction on her face other than indifference to the role he'd once played in her personal life. 'Oh, I think things worked out just fine, Eric,' she said with a casual shrug. 'I did what I had to do and you did what you had to do. Anyway, there's no point in talking about the past. You've obviously moved on, and so have I.'

The lift doors closed at that juncture, as though emphasising her point.

'You still let a good one get away,' Justin remarked on the way down. 'But your loss is my gain.'

'I thought she was only your PA,' Eric shot back.

'Oh, she *is*. But a good PA these days is worth her weight in gold. Rachel leaves the girl I had before her for dead. She's not only beautiful but bright as a button, and such a sweetie. Just think, if you two hadn't broken up Rachel would be your wife by now. Instead, she's working for me, making my life run like a breeze. Amazing the little twists and turns in life, isn't it? Aah, here we are at the lobby.'

Rachel did her best not to flinch when Justin slid a highly intimate arm around her waist and steered her smoothly from the lift in Eric and Charlotte's wake. *They* weren't touching at this point, Rachel noted. They weren't even holding hands. Charlotte's body language showed anger, and so did Eric's.

Rachel tried to be scandalised with what Justin had just done, and she was a bit, but at the same time she felt a strange elation. And some vengeful satisfaction. Now she knew what Justin had meant by putting a cat amongst the pigeons.

'I presume you're going along to the special presentation dinner tonight?' Justin asked Eric before he could make his escape with Charlotte.

'Yes, we are. Charlotte's in real estate and is here representing a wealthy client of hers.'

'I can speak for myself, Eric,' Charlotte snapped. 'Actually, my client is more than wealthy. He's a multi-multimillionaire. Trust me, if he decides to buy this place whoever you're working for won't stand a chance. What this man wants he gets. So who is it that *you* work for, anyway? And what is it that you actually do?'

Justin delivered an intriguingly enigmatic smile. 'Now, that would be telling, wouldn't it? I can confess to being an investment adviser, but, as I'm sure you are aware, client confidentiality is important in matters such as this. Property-development deals are rather like a game of poker. You don't ever put all your cards on the table, not till after the game has been done, or won.'

'My client never bluffs,' Charlotte said smugly. 'He

doesn't have to. When he wants something he simply makes sure he's the top bidder. Money overcomes all obstacles.'

'Is that so? Your client might not ever bluff, but if he keeps making business decisions that way he might end up with a house of cards rather than a solidly based portfolio. One day, it'll come crashing down around him.'

'Well, that's no concern of mine,' Charlotte said with an indifferent shrug of her slender shoulders. 'He's just a client. As long as I get my commission on a sale, I don't care what happens afterwards.'

'Spoken like a real-estate agent,' Justin said with a dry laugh.

She didn't bat an eyelid at the barb. 'Property's a tough business.'

'But you're well up to it.'

'Oh, I'm not *that* hard,' she returned. 'Not once you get to know me.' And she flashed him an almost co-quettish smile.

Rachel could not believe it. Charlotte was making a play for Justin right in front of her and Eric's eyes!

But what's new? she realised bitterly. That was what she'd done with Eric when he'd been engaged to her.

A quiet fury began to simmer within Rachel. Charlotte had seduced Eric away from her, but no way was Rachel going to let Charlotte get her claws into Justin! He might only be her boss but he was far too nice a man for the likes of that alley cat to play with.

'I hate to interrupt this conversation,' she piped up with a saccharine smile, 'but we really must be getting along, Justin. The dinner starts at eight and you promised to meet Mr Wong at the main bar at seven-fifteen. And it's way past that now.'

'You're right. See what I mean? What would I do
without her? No doubt we'll run into each other again
during the dinner. Maybe we can even sit at the same
table. Mind us a spot if you can. Meanwhile, I must
away and meet my—er—meet Mr Wong. And no,
don't ask me who he is, sweetheart,' he threw at
Charlotte, then pressed his index finger to his lips. 'Client confidentiality, remember.'

'Who the hell is Mr Wong?' he whispered to Rachel
after a sour-faced Eric grabbed Charlotte's arm and
started steering her forcibly past Reception in the di-
rection of the main conference room, the venue for the
dinner.

'No idea,' Rachel confessed. 'I made him up.'

'But why? The idea is to stay in Eric and Charlotte's
company if we're to achieve our aim for the night.'
And nodded towards the departing couple's backs.

'She was flirting with you,' Rachel pointed out in-
dignantly.

'So? That was good, wasn't it? It'll make Eric the
Mongrel jealous and insecure.'

'I was afraid you might be liking it.'

'I was. But not the way you're thinking. I wouldn't
touch that cold-blooded bitch in a million years. God,
Rachel, you don't know me very well if you'd think
that.'

'But I *don't* know you very well, do I? You have an
unexpectedly wicked streak in you, Justin McCarthy.
Yet before tonight I thought you were…um—er—er…'
She struggled to find a word other than 'nice'.

'Staid?' he suggested drily. 'Boring?'

'No! Never boring. Maybe a little staid. No, you're
not really staid, either. Oh, I don't know what I mean.
I guess I just didn't think you'd ever conceive of some-

thing so devious as to make them think we're lovers even whilst you're claiming we aren't. That was incredibly conniving of you, and manipulative.'

'If you can't beat 'em, then join 'em, Rachel. People like Eric and Charlotte are devious, and conniving, and manipulative. They're also shallow and selfish and truly wicked. They don't care who they hurt or betray. All they care about is themselves and what suits them at the time. If you think I'm the first man Charlotte has flirted with, then think again. She hasn't been faithful to your Eric, nor he with her. That's the way they both are.'

'Maybe, but not *everyone* is like that, Justin,' she pointed out, unwilling to embrace the self-destructive philosophy of total cynicism. Isabel had been like that with men for ages, till she met Rafe. And, really, Rachel hadn't admired that about her one bit. She was a much nicer person now that she was living her life with love and hope in her heart.

'True,' Justin said, his gaze softening momentarily on her. 'Some people are decent and kind. But the two people we were unfortunate enough to fall in love with *weren't*. Eric treated you abominably, Rachel. And he shouldn't be allowed to get away with it!'

Rachel stared up into her boss's bitter blue eyes and realised he wasn't only talking about Eric. He was talking—and thinking—about his wife. Justin was deeply wounded.

Rachel wanted to ask him about his wife and what she'd done to him, but knew it was not the right time, or the right place. For one thing, his wounds were still way too raw. Maybe there would never be a right time or a right place. Maybe he'd loved her far too much, and would never get over her.

At least *she* had the comfort of knowing she no longer loved Eric. Seeing him again tonight had at least proved that to her once and for all. He might be successful and superficially handsome, but 'handsome is as handsome does', she'd discovered first-hand this evening. He was welcome to the likes of Charlotte. They were made for each other, in her opinion.

'Promise me you won't flirt with Charlotte when we finally get to that dinner?' she asked.

Justin laughed. 'I promise. But you shouldn't worry about me, you know, Rachel. I can take care of myself where female vampires are concerned. How are *you* doing, meeting up with lover-boy again? Does he still turn you on with those smooth, golden looks of his?'

'God, no.' She half laughed, half shuddered. 'No, not at all.'

'I suspect he still has the hots for you.'

She blushed. 'Don't be ridiculous!'

Justin frowned. 'You think it's ridiculous for a man to have the hots for you, especially the way you look tonight?'

'Well, no... I mean...yes... I mean... Look, I still can't compare with Charlotte. She's one seriously sexy lady.'

'She's about as sexy to me as a dead skunk.'

Rachel was startled. 'Really?'

'Really. But to ease your concern I will consign all of my flirting for the rest of the evening to yours truly. Make Eric the Mongrel's teeth gnash some more.' He glanced at his watch. 'Mmm. Twenty to eight. Look, let's go to that main bar you mentioned, where I'm supposed to be meeting the mysterious Mr Wong. We can fill in the time till eight with a couple of pre-dinner drinks.'

Rachel bit her bottom lip. 'Oh, I—er—made that up about the main bar as well. I have no idea if there is such a place.'

Justin grinned. 'And you said I had an unexpectedly wicked streak in me. I think you're the one who has the unexpectedly wicked streak, Ms Witherspoon. Come on, we'll go ask at Reception where the bars are located. They have to have at least one or two in a place this size.'

They had three, one connected with the à la carte restaurant on the mezzanine level, one on the first floor in the disco-till-you-drop room and a third up on the top floor, which had a more sedate dance floor and a view to die for, or so the clerk behind the desk said. It also wasn't open to the public, just the clientele of Sunshine Gardens and their guests.

Ten minutes later they were sitting at a table on an open-air terrace, sipping Margaritas by moonlight and drinking in that view to die for, which was spectacular, even at night. Most of the buildings along the foreshore were lit up, outlining the curved sweep of the coastline for as far as the eye could see. The night air was still and balmy, with Rachel's bare arms and shoulders not proving a problem.

'This is so lovely,' she said with a wistful sigh. 'But we won't have time for a second drink. Not if you want us to make that dinner on time.'

Actually, she hated the thought of going down to that dinner now. As much as she'd enjoyed her moment of vengeance in the lift, she didn't want to keep pretending she and Justin were lovers, or to have Justin acting like some sleazebag boss who couldn't keep his hands off her. She knew he meant well, but in a way it was demeaning for him to act out of character like that.

'What if I said we'd skip the presentation dinner entirely, and order some food to have right here?' he startled her by suggesting. 'They do serve light meals. They're listed on the other side of the drinks menu.'

'But don't you *have* to go to the dinner?'

'It's not strictly essential. They're making a video of the promotional presentation after the dinner for potential buyers who couldn't make it tonight. I'll buy a copy in the morning and view it when I get home tomorrow night, in case there's anything remotely informative in it, which is doubtful.'

'But what about Eric and Charlotte?'

'What about them? You said you didn't give a toss about Eric any more.'

'I don't.'

'Well, then we've done what we set out to do,' he said. 'Made Eric the Mongrel see you've survived without him. Also made him see he gave up a truly fine and, might I say, very attractive lady for a total bitch like Charlotte. Frankly, it could prove a more successful and devious strategy not showing up to the dinner at all. Eric will stew over the thought that I've whisked you back up to our room for a long night of hot sex, and darling Charlotte will worry her material little heart out that my mysterious Mr Wong might be some mega-rich businessman from Singapore who'll bid more for Sunshine Gardens than the ego-maniacal fool she's representing. Your revenge is already complete, Rachel. Why risk spoiling it?'

'But...'

'You have a penchant for buts, Rachel. There are no buts in this case, not even business buts. I guarantee I won't get into trouble over not going to that dinner. I made my own private enquiries around town today and I won't be recommending that AWI buy this place, anyway. Reliable sources tell me the occupancy rate here is way down, except in peak tourist season, and even then not a patch on a couple of their nearby competitors. Another little birdie told me that, despite the quality of the building and the décor, the management here is less than the best and staff turnover is very high.'

'What reliable sources? What little birdie?'

'The people who live here in Coolangatta, and work here. Shop owners. Suppliers. Taxi drivers. They have no reason to lie, whereas the present owners of Sunshine Gardens have every reason to misrepresent the truth.'

'I see.'

'So what do you say? We miss the dinner and stay up here?'

'Yes, please,' Rachel said eagerly as relief overwhelmed her.

Justin smiled his own pleasure at the change of plan. 'We'll order a bottle of wine with our dinner,' he suggested on picking up the menu. 'And then we might have a dance or two. That dress has dancing written all over it.'

Rachel's heart jolted. She hadn't danced in years. The last time had been with Eric, the week before he'd broken off with her, and the day before she found out the awful news about Lettie. They'd been to a Christmas party and she'd got very tipsy on the punch. He'd whispered hot words of love and desire in her ears whilst he danced with her, holding her very close, making her want him to put his words into action.

When she'd been beyond resisting him he'd whisked her into the bathroom and made love to her up against the door.

Or so she'd thought at the time. Now she knew he hadn't been making love at all. He'd just been having sex. Because he'd never really loved her.

'I…I haven't danced in years,' she said, her voice shaking a little at the memory. As much as she no longer loved Eric, the damage he'd perpetrated on her female psyche was still there.

'You didn't dance at your friend's wedding?' Justin asked on a note of surprise.

'No.'

'Why not? I'll bet you were asked in that dress.'

'Yes, I was.'

'Why did you say no?'

'I…I just didn't want to.' In truth, she'd felt far too emotionally fragile at the time to do something as potentially destructive as dance with a man. When she'd watched the bride and groom dance their first dance together she'd been consumed with a pain so sharp, and a misery so deep, she'd fled into a powder room—one of her favourite escapes—and cried for ages.

Justin frowned. 'This has something to do with Eric the Mongrel, hasn't it?'

Her smile was sad. 'How did you guess?'

'You told him in the lift you'd moved on, Rachel. And you told me just now he no longer mattered to you. I think it's time you put your feet where your mouth is. You're going to dance with me tonight and I don't want to hear another word about it. I won't take no for an answer.'

'Yes, boss,' she said, rather amused by his tough-guy attitude. It was so un-Justin. Same as with his earlier pretending to be a sleazebag boss.

'That's a very good phrase,' he pronounced firmly. 'Practise saying it.'

'Yes, boss.'

'Again.'

She laughed. 'Yes, boss.'

He grinned. 'By George, she's got it!'

# CHAPTER SEVEN

JUSTIN sat there, watching Rachel really enjoy herself, possibly for the first time in years. She'd relished the food, despite the meal being a simple one, and she'd certainly swigged back her fair share of the wine. Now she was looking totally relaxed, leaning back and peering up at the stars.

He'd just ordered their after-dinner coffee but it probably wouldn't arrive for a while. Whilst the setting and ambience of the bar was great, the service was slow. The place was clearly understaffed, especially for a Saturday night. Management were probably cutting costs to make their profit margin look better, a common strategy when a business was for sale.

Time to ask Rachel to dance, Justin decided. The music coming from inside the bar was nice and slow, the rhythm easy to follow.

He rose to his feet, walked round her side of the table and held out his hand towards her. 'Shall we take a turn around the terrace, Ms Witherspoon?' he asked with feigned old-fashioned formality.

She smiled up at him. Such a lovely smile she had. Pity she didn't use it more often. Still, maybe she would after tonight.

'Why, thank you, Mr Darcy. Oops. Mr McCarthy, I mean.' When she stood up she swayed back dangerously on her high heels. He grabbed her upper arms and pulled her hard against him.

'Oh,' she gasped, her eyes startled as they jerked up to meet his.

'Methinks you've had too much to drink, Ms Witherspoon,' he chided gently. 'Just as well you find yourself in a gentleman's company this evening, or you might be in a spot of bother.'

'Yes. Just as well,' she murmured even whilst her eyes remained locked to his and her woman's body stayed pressed up against him.

Justin could not believe it when his own male body suddenly stirred to life. Neither could Rachel, by the look on her face.

Nevertheless, she didn't move. Or say a word. Just stared up at him with those lovely eyes of hers, her lips still parted. Yet for all that, she didn't look disgusted, or repelled by his arousal. Neither did she attempt to push him away, not even when his arms developed a devilish mind of their own and stole around her waist, one hand settling in the small of her back, the other sliding down to play over the soft swell of her buttocks. Instead of wrenching away from him in outrage, her own arms actually slipped up around his neck, and she sank even more closely against him.

'Rachel,' he breathed warningly.

'Yes, boss?' she said in a low, husky voice, her hazel eyes having gone all smoky.

'You're drunk.'

'Yes, boss.'

'Maybe dancing together isn't such a good idea.'

'Just shut up, boss, and move your feet.'

Her uncharacteristic assertiveness surprised him, but he shut up and moved his feet. Still, he'd been right. It wasn't a good idea. The slow, sensual rhythm of the music got further into his blood, as did the scent—and softness—of the woman in his arms. Of course, it didn't help that her fingertips started stroking the back of his neck in a highly provocative fashion, or that she kept gazing up at him with eyes full of erotic promise. By the time the music stopped he was in agony, his erection straining against the fly of his suit trousers.

At least he had a jacket on.

'I need to go to the gents',' he ground out after depositing her back in her chair. Fortunately, their coffee had finally arrived. A potful, as ordered. Hopefully, after a couple of strong cups Rachel might sober up and stop trying to seduce him.

His normally very proper PA was going to hate herself in the morning, Justin thought ruefully as he strode back inside the bar and over to the gents'. Alcohol could make even the most sensible woman behave a bit stupidly. Add her tipsy state to all that had happened earlier this evening, and he had a very different Rachel on his hands tonight.

Of course, he had to shelve some of the blame himself. He hadn't realised when he'd encouraged her to make herself over today that her transformation would be quite so dramatic. When a woman looked as seriously good as Rachel did tonight she was apt to find her flirtatious side.

Still, what was *his* excuse for responding so powerfully? Since he didn't fancy Rachel in that sense, he could only conclude he was suffering from acute frustration.

Maybe his male body was finally rebelling against its long stint of celibacy. Possibly it was time for him to search out an accommodating female who'd give him regular sex without any emotional strings involved. *Definitely* no strings involved. The last thing he wanted was a serious relationship. Or being told he was loved.

Definitely not. Sex was all he needed, something that was painfully obvious when he went into a cubicle in the gents' and confronted his wayward flesh.

Justin sighed and waited till the worst had subsided. But he was still aroused when he emerged from the cubicle to wash his hands. The sight of a condom dispenser on the wall next to the basins immediately caught his attention, with temptation not far behind.

Before he could think better of it, he dropped a couple of single dollars in the slot provided and slipped two condoms in his trouser pocket. Who knew? He might come back up here after Rachel was asleep. It was still only early. He'd already noticed an attractive redhead sitting all by herself at the bar, who'd given him the eye as he walked past. He just might return and take her up on her none-too-subtle invitation, since getting to sleep tonight in his present state of mind and body might prove difficult.

Difficult? More like bloody impossible!

Once Justin left her alone, Rachel's conscience—and common sense—returned with a vengeance. What on earth did she think she was doing, flirting with her boss and dancing with him like that, winding her arms around his neck like a clinging vine and moulding her body to his like some neglected nymphomaniac?

Justin's getting turned on wasn't his fault. He was just a man after all, a man who possibly hadn't had sex for some time. His leaving her to race off to the gents' had been too embarrassing for words.

Rachel cringed with humiliation, and guilt. If she could have bolted back to her hotel room right now without consequences she would have. If Justin hadn't been in possession of the door key she might have. As things stood, she had no alternative but to sit there and wait for his return, when she would apologise for her appalling behaviour, and beg his forgiveness and understanding. She would blame the wine, then throw herself on his mercy by explaining that she wasn't herself tonight.

Not her recent self, anyway. The Rachel Justin had employed would never have acted as she just had. In a way, it amazed her that she'd had the gall. Being sexually aggressive took courage, and confidence. Either that, or being turned on to the max.

This last thought bothered her the most. Because during those moments when she'd felt his hardness pressing into her stomach she'd wanted him in the most basic way; wanted to feel him, not against her but inside her. It was a startling state of affairs for a girl who'd always believed she had to be in love to want to be made love to. Clearly, she'd come to a point in her life when that wasn't the case any more. Perhaps that was what happened to a single woman when she got to a certain age, or when she'd been so lonely for so long that any man would do.

Rachel hated that idea but she could not deny it just might be true.

Crossing her arms with a shiver that had nothing to do with being cold, Rachel peered anxiously through the plate-glass window into the more dimly lit bar, both wanting and fearing Justin's return.

But there was no sign of him. He was certainly taking his time.

Desperate for distraction from her increasing agitation, she poured herself some coffee and gulped it down, black and strong. Unfortunately, this only served to sober her up and make her agonise further over the folly of her earlier actions.

She was refilling her empty cup when her boss finally showed up, but he didn't sit back down. He stayed standing by the table, his expression grim as he frowned down at her.

'I think I should take you back to the apartment,' he said abruptly. 'What you need is sleep, not coffee.'

'I'm not *that* drunk,' she replied sharply before remembering that being intoxicated was to be one of her excuses for behaving badly.

'I didn't say you were. But you've had a long and emotionally exhausting day. Come along, Rachel, be a good girl, now, and don't argue with me.'

Perversely, Rachel now felt like arguing with him, his patronising tone having really rubbed her up the wrong way. Any thought of apologising went out of the window.

He'd been equally to blame for what had just happened, she decided mutinously. If he hadn't insisted she tart herself up she would never have had the confidence to do any of the things she'd done tonight. *He'd* never have asked her to dance, either. When she'd been a plain Jane he hadn't given her a second glance.

She'd be damned if she was going to feel ashamed of her behaviour. Considering how long it had been since a man had taken her in his arms, it was no wonder she'd lost her head there for a while. She was only human.

*A soon-to-be unemployed human, if you keep this attitude up,* came the dry voice of reason.

With a sigh of surrender to common sense over rebellion, Rachel put down her coffee-cup and levered herself carefully out of the chair. This time, she was much more steady on her feet.

'I didn't think Cinderella had to go home till midnight,' she muttered with a glance at her watch. 'It's only half-past ten. Still, if you say it's time for me to go to bed then it's time for me to go to bed. You're the boss after all.'

Justin wished she hadn't said that, his mind immediately filling with various lust-filled scenarios associated with his taking this particular Cinderella to bed, none of which involved his playing the role of Prince Charming. More like the Black Prince. When he went to take her arm he thought better of it, deciding to keep his hands to himself till she was safely ensconced in her bedroom. *Alone.*

'Let's go, then,' he grated out, and stepped back to wave her ahead of him.

Unfortunately, Rachel walking ahead of him in that highly provocative dress stimulated him further. If she'd had eyes in the back of her head she'd have been disgusted by his suddenly lascivious gaze as it gobbled up her rear view, which, whilst not quite as delicious as her front, had the bonus of its owner not being aware of being ogled. He could ogle to his heart's content.

Justin didn't even notice the redhead at the bar this time as he passed by, his attention all on Rachel's *derrière* in motion. The tinkling sounds of the crystal-drop hem brushing against her legs dragged his eyes down to her shapely calves, then further down to her slender ankles and sexily shod feet.

Justin didn't normally have a shoe or foot fetish, but that didn't stop him imagining Rachel walking in front of him in nothing but those turquoise high heels. Nothing. Not a stitch.

His stomach crunched down hard at the mental image, blood roaring round his body and gathering in his nether regions. The end result was an erection like Mount Vesuvius on the boil. It surprised him that there wasn't smoke wafting from his trousers.

Their ride down in the lift was awkward and silent, Justin keeping his hands linked loosely over his groin area in a seemingly nonchalant attitude, but inside he was struggling with the most corrupting thoughts.

She probably wouldn't stop you if you started making love to her. She wants it. You know she does. Understandable under the circumstances. She probably hasn't been to bed with a man since Eric the Mongrel left her. And she certainly hasn't looked this good since then, either. She wants you to want her. That's why she was stroking your neck like that. And that's why she wasn't all that happy a minute ago when you brought her Cinderella night to an abrupt halt. You'd be doing her a favour if you slept with her. You'd be delivering the whole fantasy. A man in her bed for the night. A man wanting her again. A man finding her beautiful and desirable and, yes, sexy.

Which he did find her tonight. What man wouldn't? She looked gorgeous.

But what about in the morning, Justin? What about next week when you have to work with her? What then?

Justin smothered a groan. He couldn't do it. No matter what. It was unacceptable and unconscionable and just plain wrong. She might not be dead drunk but she was decidedly tipsy, and extra-vulnerable tonight. She needed compassion, not passion. Understanding, not underhanded tactics.

'You're angry with me, aren't you?' she said wretchedly when they finally made it into the apartment, neither having said a word since they'd left the bar.

Justin sighed. 'No, Rachel, I'm not angry with you.'

'You're acting as though you are.'

'I'm sorry if it looks that way. If you must know, I'm angry with myself.'

She blinked her surprise. 'But why? I'm the one who's been behaving badly.'

'That's a matter of opinion. If you could see into my head right now then you wouldn't think that.'

She stared at him and he stared right back, his conscience once again raging a desperate war with his fiercely aroused body. He tried to recapture the gentle and platonic feelings Rachel usually engendered in him; tried to recall how she'd once looked. But it was a losing battle. That sexless creature was gone, and in her place was this incredibly desirable woman. All he could think about was how she'd felt in his arms upstairs and how she'd feel in his bed down here.

'This is an even worse idea than dancing with you,' he muttered as he stepped forward and cupped her startled face with his hands. 'But I haven't the will-power to resist. Don't say no to me, Rachel. Not tonight.'

He was going to kiss her, Rachel realised with a small gasp of shock. No, not just kiss her. He was going to make love to her.

She almost blurted out 'no', his carnal intentions fuelling instant panic. But before her mouth could form any protest his lips had covered hers in a kiss of such hunger and intensity that she was totally blown away.

His tongue stabbed deep, his fingers sliding up into her hair, his fingertips digging into her scalp as he held her mouth solidly captive under his. It was a brutally ravaging, wildly primitive, hotly demanding kiss.

And she loved it, her moans echoing a dazed, dizzying pleasure.

'No, don't,' she choked out ambiguously when his head lifted at long last, leaving her mouth feeling bruised and bereft. She actually meant, No, don't stop. But he naturally took it another way.

'I told you not to say that,' he growled, and swept her up into his arms. 'There will be no ''no''s tonight.'

He kissed her again as he carried her down to his room, then kissed her some more whilst he took off all her clothes. Once she was totally, shockingly naked, he spread her out on the bed and kissed every intimate erogenous part of her body.

And she never once said no. Because she never said a word. She was beyond words. Beyond anything but moaning with pleasure.

Yet she didn't come. He seemed to know just how much she could endure without tipping over the edge. Time and time again she would come incredibly close, and tense up in expectation of imminent release. But each time he would stop doing what he was doing, and she'd groan and writhe with frustration. As often as not he'd just smile down at her, as though he was enjoying her torment.

By the time he deserted her to strip off all his own clothes she would have done anything he asked. But he didn't ask. Instead, he drew on one of the two condoms he pulled from his trouser pocket, and just took. Swiftly and savagely.

'Oh,' Rachel gasped, coming within seconds of his

entering her. She'd never climaxed as quickly as that before, her flesh gripping his as he continued to thrust wildly into hers. He didn't last long, either, his back arching as his mouth gaped wide in a naked cry of primal release. Afterwards, he collapsed across her, his chest heaving, his breathing raw.

Rachel just lay there under him, stunned and confused. For a woman whose body had just been racked by a fierce and fantastic orgasm, she didn't feel at all satisfied, just primed for more.

'Don't talk,' he commanded when he finally withdrew and scooped her still turned-on body up in his arms. 'Talking will only spoil everything.'

His *en suite* bathroom was as white and spacious as hers, with a shower cubicle built for two. Holding her with one strong arm, he adjusted the water on both shower heads then deposited her in there before leaving to attend to the condom.

Rachel stood under the warm water and watched him through the clear glass of the shower cubicle, thinking that he really had a fabulous body. When he'd undressed earlier she'd been too caught up with her own excitement and apprehension to notice him in detail. Now her eyes avidly drank in his perfect male shape; the broad shoulders, slender hips, tight buttocks. Muscles abounded in his back, arms and legs. He also sported an all-over tan, except for the area that had been covered by a very brief swimming costume. Justin was built very well indeed. His wife certainly hadn't left him because he was inadequate in that department. Or in the lovemaking department either. He knew what to do with a woman's body all right. He made Eric's idea of foreplay look pathetically inadequate.

Thinking of Justin's wife and Eric reminded Rachel

that what she was doing here—and what Justin was doing here—had nothing to do with love and relationships, and everything to do with need. Need for sex, and the need to be needed, even if only sexually.

At least, that was the way it was for her. Justin's wanting her, even for this one night, had done more for her feminine self-esteem than all the physical makeovers in the world. He'd brought out the woman in her again. If nothing else, after tonight she could not go back to being that pretend plain Jane who'd been playing the role of his prim PA in such a piteous fashion.

Even if it meant having to resign, she would truly move on from this point, and live her life as she once had. There would be no more wimpishly making the least of herself. No more hiding behind dreary black suits and spinsterish hairdos. Definitely no more being afraid of other people, and men in particular. That sad, lonely chapter in her life was over.

'You're thinking,' Justin grumbled as he joined her under the water and turned up the hot tap.

'And you're talking,' she reminded him as she lifted her hands to slick her dripping hair back from her face.

'That's my prerogative. I'm the boss. Keep your arms up and your hands behind your head like that,' he ordered thickly. 'Lock your fingers together. Keep your elbows back.'

Rachel was staggered by his request. But she obeyed, and found the experience an incredible turn-on. By the look in his eyes, Justin did too. His gaze roved hotly over her body, which felt extra-naked and extra-exposed as she stood there like that. The now steaming water kept splashing over her head and running down her face, into the corners of her by now panting mouth. Down her neck it streamed, forming a rivulet between her breasts, pooling in her navel before spilling down to the juncture between her thighs, soaking the curl-covered mound and finally finding its way into the already hot, wet valleys of her female flesh.

'Beautiful,' he murmured, his voice low and taut. 'Now close your eyes and don't talk. Or move.'

Her eyes widened but then fluttered closed, as ordered. Rachel was far too excited to even consider not obeying him. She'd never played erotic games before, and the experience was blowing her mind.

Now, within her self-imposed prison of darkness, she could only imagine how she looked, standing there so submissively, with her elbows back and her breasts thrust forward, their nipples achingly erect. Was he looking at her and despising her for her unexpected wantonness, or delighting in her willingness to play slave to his master?

The shocking part was she didn't seem to care, as long as he looked, and touched, and satisfied her once more. By the time his hands started skimming lightly over her body, she was already craving another climax, her mind propelling her forward to that moment when he'd surge up into her, filling her, fulfilling her.

She moaned softly when something—not his hand—rubbed over her nipples. Soap, she soon realised. A cake of soap. He wasn't washing her as such, just using the soap, caressing her with its slippery surface, making her nipples tighten even further. Every internal muscle she owned tightened along with them. When the soap started travelling southwards Rachel sucked in sharply.

No, not there, she wanted to warn him. But before her tongue could formulate her brain's protest the soap was between her legs, sliding back and forth, back and forth, back and forth. She tried to stop the inevitable

## The Reader Service™ — Here's how it works:

NO STAMP
NEEDED!

THE READER SERVICE™
FREE BOOK OFFER
FREEPOST CN81
CROYDON
CR9 3WZ

If offer card is missing write to: The Reader Service, PO Box 236, Croydon, CR9 3RU

NO STAMP
NECESSARY
IF POSTED IN
THE U.K. OR N.I.

# GET FREE BOOKS
## and a
# FREE GIFT WHEN YOU PLAY THE...

# LAS VEGAS
## GAME

*Just scratch off the gold box
with a coin. Then check
below to see the gifts you get!*

◄ DETACH AND POST CARD TODAY! ►

# YES!
I have scratched off the gold box. Please send me my
**2 FREE BOOKS** and gift for which I qualify. I understand that
I am under no obligation to purchase any books as explained on
the back of this card. I am over 18 years of age.

P3AI

Mrs/Miss/Ms/Mr _____ Initials _____

BLOCK CAPITALS PLEASE

Surname _____

Address _____

_____

Postcode _____

| 7 | 7 | 7 | Worth TWO FREE BOOKS plus a BONUS Gift! |
| 🍒 | 🍒 | 🍒 | Worth TWO FREE BOOKS! |
| 🔔 | 🔔 | ♣ | TRY AGAIN! |

Visit us online at

www.millsandboon.co.uk

from happening, but it was like trying to stop a ski-jumper in mid-jump. When her belly grew taut and her thighs began to tremble she knew the struggle for control had been futile.

She came with a violent rush, her knees going to jelly and her arms falling back down to her sides. She might have sunk into a wet heap on the floor had he not snapped off the water and swept her back up into his arms. Her eyes must have conveyed her shocked state as he carried her back to his bedroom, but he just ignored them and spread her dripping body face down across the bed, pushing a pillow up under her hips.

Was she too shattered to stop him at that moment? Or was this what she secretly wanted as well? For him to take her like that. For him to take her over and over in every position imaginable. To make her come again and again. To show her…what?

That she could be as wickedly sexy as the next woman? As Charlotte, perhaps?

When he didn't touch her—or take her—straight away an impatient Rachel glanced over her shoulder, only to see he was busy with a condom. She was tempted to tell him that he didn't really have to use protection. Not unless he was a health risk. Perversely, she was on the Pill for reasons which had nothing to do with contraception. It simply stopped her from having dreadful PMT, which she hadn't been able to cope with on top of the stress of minding Lettie.

She didn't tell him, in the end. Not right then. She wasn't *that* brazen. But she told him later, after she realised he had no more condoms and she'd moved way beyond brazen, way beyond anything she thought she could ever be.

# CHAPTER EIGHT

Justin stared down at the sleeping woman in his bed with disbelieving eyes. Was that really his prim and proper PA lying there in the nude, looking wickedly sexy with a sheet pulled suggestively up between her legs? And had it been himself who'd ravaged and ravished her amazingly co-operative body all night long?

The answer was yes, to both questions.

He groaned, his hands lifting to clap each side of his face then rake up into his hair. Whatever had possessed him? With Rachel, of all women!

Bosses who seduced their secretaries were top of his most despised list of men.

But seduce Rachel he had. The fact that she'd enjoyed herself enormously in the end had little bearing on the fact that initially he'd taken advantage of her drunken and vulnerable state, blatantly using his position as her boss to pressure her into sex. When he thought of the things he'd asked her to do in the shower his mind boggled. That she'd done everything he wanted, without question, was testament to her not being her usual sensible self. It was a particularly telling moment when she'd confessed later in the night to being on the Pill. No girl these days made such a rash revelation, not unless they were totally out of their minds with lust!

Which Rachel had been by then. No doubt about it.

Astonishing, really. He would never have believed it of her. Not with him, anyway. Still, given the circumstances, possibly any man would have done last night. He'd known that subconsciously. Hell, no, he'd known it *consciously*. He'd thought about her vulnerable state *before* he'd crossed the line. And what had he done? Still crossed that line, then wallowed in her unexpected sensuality and insatiability, urging her on to arouse him repeatedly with her mouth till he was ready to take her in yet another erotically challenging position.

His body stirred just thinking about it. Groaning, Justin dragged his eyes away from Rachel's tempting nudity and headed straight for the bathroom, plunging his wayward flesh into the coldest of showers.

She'll have to go, he began thinking, despite the icy spray doing the trick. I can't possibly work with her. She'll make me feel guilty all the time. Or worse.

The prospect of spending every weekday having cold showers at lunch time would be untenable. Aside from the constant distraction and frustration, it would remind him of Mandy, and what Mandy was up to on a daily basis with that bastard boss of hers.

Yet to sack Rachel would make him an even bigger bastard of a boss. Justin was trapped by the situation. Damned if he did and damned if he didn't!

'Bloody hell,' he muttered, and slammed his palms hard against the wet tiles.

Rachel woke with a start, her eyes blinking as she tried to focus on where she was. She didn't recognise the ceiling. Or the walls. Or the bed, for that matter.

And then, suddenly, she remembered.

Everything.

'Oh, God,' she moaned.

The sound of the shower running was some comfort,

because it gave Rachel the opportunity to jump out of the bed, gather up her clothes and escape back to her own room without having to face Justin, naked, in his bed.

Grimacing, she dived into a shower of her own without delay, where she stayed for some time, doing her best to wash away all the evidence of what she could only describe as a night best forgotten.

But forgetting the way she'd acted was nigh on impossible when she was constantly confronted with the physical consequences of her amazingly decadent behaviour. Her nipples ached. Her mouth felt like suede. And she probably wouldn't be able to walk without discomfort for a week.

As much as she hadn't felt ashamed of her behaviour last night—she'd blindly viewed it as an exciting liberation from her drab, lonely and celibate existence—in the cold light of day she could see that having her own private orgy with her boss had not been a good career move.

He would not be pleased, she knew, either with her or himself.

Rachel was sitting on the side of her bed half an hour later and wishing she were dead, when a knock on the door made her jump.

'Rachel,' Justin said through the door in a businesslike voice. 'Are you dressed?'

'Not quite,' she croaked out. A lie, since she'd just pulled on an outfit from Isabel's discarded resort wardrobe, white capri pants and a matching white and yellow flowered top, *with* underwear, thank God. She'd bought a couple of bra and pants sets the previous day. But her hair was still wrapped in a towel and she hadn't a scrap of make-up on.

Despite regretting going to bed with Justin, no way was she going to revert to plain-Jane mode again. If nothing else, yesterday's make-over had propelled her out of that pathetic state.

'We have to talk,' Justin went on. 'And we have to eat. In case you haven't noticed, it's after eleven and the breakfast buffet downstairs has long closed.'

'I'm not very hungry,' she said wretchedly.

'Maybe not, but you still have to eat something. We'll only get a snack on the flight home this afternoon. Look, why don't I order sandwiches from Room Service whilst you get dressed? Then we can talk over brunch on the terrace. We have plenty of coffee and tea in the room, so a hot drink is no problem. See you out on the terrace in, say...half an hour?'

'All right,' she agreed, thinking with some relief how very civilised he was sounding. Maybe he wasn't going to sack her after all.

Any hope of Justin's that she might appear dressed in dreary black again was dashed when she stepped out onto the terrace looking delicious in tight white trousers and a bright yellow top that hugged her breasts. For a girl he'd recently thought of as skinny, she had some surprising curves.

And some surprising moves, he recalled, doing his best not to stare at her pink glossed mouth.

Gritting his teeth, he waved her to her seat at the table, then got straight down to brass tacks. No point in putting off the unpleasant.

'Before you say anything,' he began, 'let me immediately apologise for my appalling behaviour last night. I have few excuses, except possibly eighteen months of celibacy and half a bottle of wine. Then, of course, there was the way you looked last night…' Not to mention the way you look this morning, he could have added when his gaze swept over her again.

On top of the figure-fitting clothes, her hair was swinging around her face in a sleek, sexy red curtain, and her scarlet-painted toes were peeping out at him from her open-toed white sandals. She also smelled like fresh green apples, a scent he'd always liked.

'I owe you an apology as well,' she returned with what sounded like relief in her voice. 'I led you on when we danced together. I know I did. And I certainly didn't say no at any stage. I guess I must have been drunker than I realised.'

Justin was happy to play it that way, if it made her feel better. It certainly made him feel better. Or did it? Was she implying she must have been plastered to go to bed with him? Did she need reminding just how many times she'd come last night? And how often she'd begged him not to stop, long after the effects of that wine had worn off?

She'd been drunk all right. Drunk on desire.

*You wanted me, baby,* was on the tip of his tongue.

But, of course, he didn't say that.

'Fine,' he said instead. 'We're both to blame. That's fair. So let's forgive each other, forget last night ever happened and just go on as before.'

He saw her shoulders snap back against the seat and her chin jerk up in surprise. She fixed frowning eyes upon him. 'You can really do that? Forget last night ever happened?'

*Not with you sitting next to me, sweetheart. And looking good enough to eat.*

Justin shrugged. 'Yes, why not? It didn't mean anything to either of us. You needed a man and I needed a woman. It was simply a case of being in the wrong place at the wrong time. It's obvious that both of us need to get out more,' he finished up with a bitter little smile.

'So you're not going to sack me?'

'Sack you! Of course not. The thought never occurred to me.'

Which was possibly only the first of a host of lies he'd be telling Rachel in future.

'I...I was worried that you might. Isabel always says that to have an affair with the boss is the kiss of death, job-wise. The girl always ends up being given the boot.'

Not always, he wanted to say. Not when the woman in question is my beautiful blonde ex-wife. She's been her boss's assistant-cum-mistress for two years and they're still together, at it like rabbits on desks and in private jets and on yacht decks.

'But we're not having an affair, are we?' he reminded Rachel ruefully. 'We made the mistake of going to bed together. *Once.* But we won't be making that mistake again, will we?'

'What? Oh, no. No, certainly not,' she said firmly, but her eyes remained worryingly ambivalent.

Justin knew then that she was experiencing at least a little of the leftover feelings which were still haunting him.

Damn, damn and double damn! His own dark desires he could cope with. And hide. But he was a goner if she started coming on to him again.

'One thing, though,' he went on brusquely.

'Yes?'

'Your appearance...'

'Yes?'

Justin wasn't sure if what he was about to say would work. But it was the only way out of the bind he'd got himself into.

'I—er—wondered if you're intending to dress differently for work from now on. I mean…I'm only human, Rachel, and I wouldn't want you coming into the office in clothes which I might find…distracting.'

She closed her eyes for a few seconds and pursed her pretty lips. 'Justin…' Her eyes opened again and her chin lifted in what could only be described as a defiant gesture. 'I'm sorry,' she said firmly, 'but I refuse to go back to the way I used to look. I couldn't. I'd rather resign than do that.'

'There is no question of your resigning!' he pronounced heatedly. Surprising, when this was what he'd been trying to make her do. Resign. But the moment she said she might he knew that was not what he wanted. He wanted Rachel to stay on, working for him. He wanted… God, he didn't know what he wanted any more.

He smothered a weary sigh before it left his lungs. 'You can wear what you like,' he said. 'Within reason, of course.'

'I've *never* been the type of girl to dress provocatively at work, Justin. I simply won't be wearing those awful black suits again, except perhaps tomorrow. I don't have any other work clothes till I buy some more. I'll pop out and buy a couple of brighter outfits during my lunch hour.'

'Not too bright, I hope,' he muttered, dreading anything which would constantly draw his eyes and rev up his hormones. 'What about your hair?'

'What about it? Don't tell me it's too bright as well.'

No, just too damned sexy the way you're wearing it today.

'Would you consider wearing it back up again?' he suggested in desperation. 'I've always thought that a suitable look for work.'

She sighed. 'Very well, I'll put my hair up.'

'And not too much make-up.'

'I have *never* worn too much make-up, either. I only have lipstick on at this moment.'

'Really?'

He would have sworn she was wearing much more. Her skin looked so pale and clear, yet her cheeks were glowing. As for her eyes... He'd always known they were her best feature but had they always had such long lashes?

'Don't worry, Justin,' she said with more than a touch of irritation in her voice. 'I won't waltz in to work looking like the office slut. And I promise I'll wear underwear.'

His stomach jolted at the thought of her walking around the office without anything on underneath her clothes. What a shockingly appealing idea!

Justin suppressed a sigh and wondered how long it would be before Rachel stopped being the object of his sexual fantasies. A week? A month? A year?

Damn, but he wished he'd resisted temptation last night. And he wished he'd never suggested that bloody make-over. He wanted his old Rachel back. She didn't stir his blood or challenge his conscience. She was sweet and kind and calming. This new Rachel was anything but calming. Even now, he wanted to say to hell with all this conciliatory chit-chat, let's just go back to bed and stay there all day. And to hell with underwear in the office as well. I *want* you buck-naked under your clothes. And no bra. Never a bra. I want your beautiful breasts accessible to my touch at the flick of a button. I want to be able to lift your skirt at any time and lean you over my desk and just do it. I want...

Justin's fantasies were really running away with him when a sudden appalling realisation reined them in. What he wanted to do with Rachel was exactly the sort of thing Mandy's rapacious boss had been doing with her!

Justin's blood ran cold at the thought, which was good. Very good. And very effective.

His burgeoning arousal ebbed away immediately.

That was what he'd do in future. Think of Mandy whenever these unacceptable desires struck. Pity he hadn't thought of the bitch last night. But better later than never!

Rachel realised that her attempt at a little joke about her underwear had backfired when Justin's back stiffened and his face took on an icily disapproving expression. Truly! It was getting difficult to remember him as the red-hot lover who'd made her do all the deliciously wicked things he'd made her do last night.

All of a sudden, he was acting like some prude!

Still, maybe that was what he basically was. A prude. Maybe he *had* been drunker last night than he seemed at the time.

Whatever, it was clear he deeply regretted having sex with her and was doing his level best to return their relationship to its previous professional-only status, even going so far as to want her to go back to looking much the same as she used to.

Fat chance of that, buster, she thought with private mutiny. If you want me to revert to plain-Jane mode, how about you doing something about *your* looks?

Why don't you stack on twenty kilos, and put a paper bag over your head for good measure? Oh, and start wearing grotty, nerdy clothes, none of those super-suave suits you wear into the office, or that coolly casual outfit you've got on at the moment. After all, sexual attraction—and distraction—was a two-way thing.

From the moment she'd set eyes on him again this morning, her heart had quickened and her eyes had surreptitiously gobbled him up. Frankly, it had been an effort so far not to keep staring at him in those smart beige trousers and that sexy black open-necked shirt. She supposed she should be grateful that he wasn't wearing shorts, but she was still brutally aware of what lay beneath his clothes. All that working out in the gym had produced a fantastic body. Talk about toned and honed! She hadn't been able to stop touching it last night.

In fact, she *hadn't* stopped touching it. If truth be told, she wanted to touch it again. Right now.

Rachel gave herself a savage mental shake and rose to her feet.

'I'll make us some coffee to go with this food,' she said, glancing resignedly at the two plates of mixed sandwiches that were sitting on the table. She still didn't have any appetite and would definitely need help in washing bread down her throat.

'You don't have to wait on me,' he said curtly, and rose to his feet as well. 'I'll help.'

Getting the coffee together was awkward. When Justin brushed her arm Rachel jumped away as though she'd been stung by a bee. When he glared at her she winced inside.

Lord, but she was like a cat on a hot tin roof around him. The lightest of touches and her skin felt scalded.

Rachel could only hope that time would lessen this sudden and intense physical awareness. After all, last night *was* still fresh in her mind. And her body was still harbouring some solid reminders as well. She felt tender in some places and rock-hard in others. On top of that, her whole system was suffering from a general feeling of agitation, which was perverse, since all that sex should at least have relaxed her nerves, not fired them up.

Hopefully, things would improve when they were back into their normal working-day routine. It wasn't helping that they were still alone together in this hotel, well away from their real lives. Perhaps that was another reason why they'd both acted so out of character last night. A romantic setting was well-known for undermining people's sexual defences. A woman's, anyway.

Rachel's hand shook as she picked up her cup and saucer, some coffee slopping into the saucer. Justin shot her another impatient look, which irked her considerably.

'OK, so I'm clumsy this morning,' she snapped. 'We can't all be perfect all the time.'

'I would have thought that was obvious after last night,' he retorted, and carried his coffee back to the terrace without spilling a drop.

Rachel fumed as she followed. What a pig, she began thinking. And she'd always imagined him to be kind. Why, he was nothing but a typical male. Trying to put the blame on her for last night. He'd been the one to kiss her first! He was the one to open Pandora's box. And now he was trying to shove her back in there again and close the lid.

Well, she was not going to go. She was free now.

Free of Eric. Free of the past. Free to be the woman she wanted to be.

Which was not some mealy-mouthed creature who was too afraid to speak up or be herself lest she lose her job. There were plenty more PA positions to be had. And plenty more men out there who could turn her on. She didn't need Justin McCarthy to provide her with either a salary *or* sex.

Despite her disgruntled state, Rachel decided that in deference to having to tolerate Justin's constant company for the next few hours, she would hold her tongue for today. But, come tomorrow, if he started pressuring her to be something she wasn't she'd start looking around for another job.

Because there was no going back after this. The die had been cast and she intended to roll with it!

# CHAPTER NINE

JUSTIN could not believe it when he walked into work the following morning—a cowardly half an hour late— and found Rachel wearing what he'd always thought her dreariest black suit, yet looking so sexy, it was sinful.

The severely tailored jacket with its long sleeves and lapelled neckline seemed tighter, and more shapely, hugging her small waist and full breasts. Had she taken it in at the seams? She'd definitely taken the skirt up, he realised when she brought in his morning coffee, the hem now a couple of inches above her knees instead of sedately covering them. And she was wearing black stockings. Not the thick, opaque, sexless kind. The sheer, silky, sexy kind which drew a man's eye and made him picture them attached to suspenders.

When he started wondering just that he wrenched his eyes back up to her face, which wasn't much help. OK, so she *had* put her hair up, as he'd requested. But not the way she'd used to, scraped back severely into a knot. It was caught up very loosely with a long black easily removable clip. Several strands had already escaped its ineffectual clasp to curve around her chin, drawing his gaze to her mouth, a mouth which bore no resemblance to Rachel's usual workaday mouth. It was more like that mouth which had tormented and teased him on Saturday night. Blood-red and full and tempting. Oh, so incredibly tempting.

Justin clenched his teeth hard in his jaw and dropped

his gaze back to his work. 'Just put the coffee down there, thank you, Rachel,' he said brusquely, nodding to a spot near his right hand.

When she lingered in front of his desk without saying a word he was finally forced to look up. 'Yes?' he said sharply. 'What is it?'

'Could I have a longer lunch hour than usual today, Justin?' she asked. 'I have some clothes shopping to do. I'll work late to make up for it.'

Justin no longer cared what clothes she bought. She couldn't look any sexier to him if she tried, anyway.

'Yes, yes.' He waved her off impatiently. 'Take all the time you need.' *The rest of my life, preferably.*

'Are you sure?'

'Yes, Rachel,' he bit out. 'Quite sure. Now, if you'll excuse me, I have to write this report for Guy.'

'Did I hear my name mentioned?' the man himself said as he strode in.

Justin welcomed the distraction. 'Aah. You're back from Melbourne earlier than I expected,' he said, glad to have an excuse to ignore Rachel. 'How's your father?'

'Much better. It was one of those nasty viruses. He was rotten on Friday and Saturday but on the improve by yesterday. So what did you think of Sunshine Gardens?'

'Take a seat and I'll tell you. Close the door as you go out, would you, Rachel?'

Justin noticed that Guy's eyes followed her as she did so.

He gave a low whistle after the door clicked shut. 'So that's your new PA,' he said, with meaning in his voice. 'You lucky dog, you. I *love* pretty women in black. Though, of course, I prefer them in nothing at all.'

'There's nothing between Rachel and myself,' Justin lied staunchly, his face a stony mask.

Guy chuckled. 'That's your story and you're going to stick to it. Wise man. Office affairs are best kept behind closed doors. And hotel-room doors. So how was your weekend junket? Everything to your satisfaction?' And he grinned lecherously.

Justin decided to ignore Guy's none-too-subtle innuendoes and plunged into giving him a brisk report on the hotel as a property investment. Naturally, he didn't mention their not having been to the presentation dinner. He let Guy think they had. Justin had watched the video last night and hadn't changed his mind about the place, despite the glowing marketing spiel.

'So that's my professional opinion,' Justin finished up. 'Added to the fact I think it's a lemon, I also gleaned some valuable inside information from a lady real-estate agent there for the free weekend. Apparently, the client she was representing is intent on purchasing the hotel at any price. I never think it's a good idea to get into a bidding war with that kind of buyer.'

'This agent could have been bluffing.'

'Yes, but I don't think so.'

'Mmm. Do you happen to know who this interested party is?'

'No. Just that he's filthy rich and has an ego the size of his cheque-book.'

'I heard a whisper that Carl Toombs is thinking of going into the property market up that way.'

Justin struggled to keep his face unreadable. No one at AWI knew the circumstances behind his divorce. No one knew that his ex-wife was Carl Toombs' secret mistress. No one except him and Mandy and his mother.

Justin's own ego had kept their secret for them.

So of course he could not be seen to react to Carl Toombs' name in any way other than a professional one.

'The man certainly fits the description the agent gave of him,' he said coolly. 'She said her client always gets what he wants, money no object.'

And wasn't that the truth? He'd set his sights on a married woman who'd been deeply in love with her husband at the time—Justin still believed that—and totally corrupted her, with his money, his charisma and his supposed sexual prowess.

Justin hated the man with a passion. As did quite a lot of other people in Australia, people who'd invested in some of his previous entrepreneurial get-rich-quick schemes. Some had succeeded, but a good few had failed. Yet somehow Toombs always managed to extricate himself with his own fortune intact. He had brilliant lawyers and accountants, and the best of contacts, both in the political and social scene. Married twice, with an adult daughter from his first marriage and two teenage sons from his present wife, Carl Toombs was in his early fifties, but looked a lot younger, courtesy of his personal dietician, trainer and cosmetic surgeon.

When Mandy had first gone to work for Carl Toombs she'd made jokes about his vanity and massive ego. Justin had joined in. But the joke had been on Justin in the end. Carl Toombs had come out on top. Literally.

Thinking about that swine and Mandy inevitably put Justin in a foul mood. 'I hope Toombs buys the place,' he went on testily. 'And I hope he loses a packet. Of his own money for a change.'

Guy looked taken aback. 'Sounds as if you lost some of your money in one of his famous ventures.'

Justin gritted his teeth. He'd lost something he valued much more than money. 'Let's just say he wouldn't want to meet me in a dark alley on a dark night.'

Guy laughed. 'And there I've been, thinking you'd never put a foot wrong financially.'

'We all make mistakes, Guy. That's how we learn.'

'And what did tangling with Toombs teach you?'

'Never to underestimate a man who has more money than I have.'

'True,' Guy said, nodding sagely. 'OK, so you don't suggest that I recommend Sunshine Gardens to the CEO.'

'Not if you value your job.'

Guy laughed, then stood up. 'See you tomorrow morning at the gym?'

'Absolutely.'

'Don't work too hard.'

'You don't really mean that.'

Guy smiled. 'Nope. I hope you work your butt off. Profits have been up since you came here. I even sleep at night sometimes.'

'Get out of here. And tell Rachel to bring me another coffee when you go past, will you? This one's gone cold.'

'Will do. I might stay and watch her do it, too. That girl has an incredible walk. And a *derrière* to die for. But I suspect you already know that, McCarthy,' he threw over his shoulder as he walked towards the door. 'No wonder you work out every morning till you're ready to drop. Can't be easy keeping your hands off that nice piece of skirt out here.'

Justin groaned. 'For pity's sake, Guy, keep your voice down. She might hear you. Haven't you heard of sexual harassment in the workplace?'

Guy shrugged and put his hand on the door knob, but he didn't turn it. 'I could be mistaken, mate, but I caught a glimpse of something in your PA's very lovely eyes a few minutes ago which indicated she might not be averse to a little sexual harassment from you.'

'Don't be ridiculous!'

'I'm not being ridiculous. I studied body language when I did a sales and marketing course recently, and she fancies you, mate. I guarantee it. But I guess if you're not interested, then you're not interested. Poor girl. I guess she'll just have to go find herself some other tall, dark, handsome jerk to give her a bit. Pity I don't fit the bill. I'd give her one, I can tell you. OK, OK, you don't have to say it. Get lost. And I won't forget the coffee on my way out.'

He didn't. Unfortunately. Soon, Rachel was undulating towards his desk with the coffee and Justin found himself mentally stripping her again. Oh, God. This was how it all began back there in that bar, with him watching her walk in front of him and imagining her without any clothes on. The trouble was, this time he *knew* what she looked like without any clothes on. And the reality far surpassed the fantasy his imagination had conjured up. She was all woman. And she could be all his, according to Guy.

Was he right? Did she really fancy him, not as some rebound substitute for Eric the Mongrel, but as a man in his own right? Was she secretly hoping he'd keep their affair going?

The thought both excited and worried him. He didn't love her. He'd never love her. He wasn't capable of that kind of love any more. He wasn't capable of any relationship of any depth. All he would want—or need—from any woman for a long time was what she'd given him the other night. Sex without strings.

He watched her put the coffee down then glance up at him, her face expectant. 'Is that all for now?'

Was it? What would she do, he wondered, if he told her to go close the door, then lock it?

A shudder of self-loathing—or was it arousal?—ricocheted through him. He could not do it. *Would* not.

'Rachel…'

'Yes?'

'Nothing,' he bit out. 'That's all. You can get back to your work. Oh, and you can take the whole afternoon off for your shopping, if you like.'

'The whole afternoon?' she echoed in surprise.

'Yes, why not? You deserve it after the weekend.'

He'd meant she deserved some time off because, technically, she'd been working overtime. But when her face darkened he immediately saw how his words could be interpreted.

'You mean in exchange for services rendered?' she threw at him.

'No, of course not. Look, if you're going to bring that up all the time, I'm not sure we *can* go on working together.'

Justin didn't need to have studied body language to gauge her reaction to that charming little announcement. Her whole body stiffened, and her eyes…her eyes stabbed him right in the heart.

'I see,' she said frostily. 'It's nice to know where things stand. You'll have my resignation on your desk *before* I leave at lunch time. And yes, I will have the whole afternoon off, thank you very much.' Spinning on her heels, she stalked from the room, banging the door behind her.

Justin slumped back into his chair with a groan. He'd done it now. And he'd never felt lower in all his life. He dropped his head into his hands and called himself every name under the sun.

Rachel could not sit down at her desk and go calmly back to work. She paced the outer office for a couple of angry minutes, then marched into the tea room and poured herself a fresh coffee, more for something to do than because she wanted it. In fact, the steaming mug remained untouched on the counter whilst she just stood there, tapping her foot and trying to gather herself.

Isabel had been so right about office affairs. Not that she needed her best friend to tell her that. Hadn't it always been the case in the workplace? The male boss got away with sleeping around and the female employee got the push.

She had an urge to go back in there and give Justin a piece of her mind. But pride wouldn't let her. Pride and common sense. Given her lack of recent work experience, she needed a reference. Not that Justin would dare not give her a reference. She could make real trouble for him over this, if she had a mind to.

But Rachel had no stomach for such an action. No, she would simply resign and to hell with Justin McCarthy. In fact, to hell with him for the rest of the day. She was going to write out her resignation right now and leave. And then she was going to go out and spend every cent in her savings account on a brand-new wardrobe!

Leaving her coffee still untouched, Rachel stormed back to her desk and set to work on her resignation letter.

Justin was in front of one of his many computer screens, pretending to work, when his office door was flung open and Rachel marched in with flushed cheeks and her head held high.

'There's my resignation,' she announced, and slapped a typed page down in front of him. 'I'll work out my notice and I'll expect a glowing reference, though lord knows how I'm going to explain leaving my present position after so short a time. But I guess that's my problem. Oh, and I'm taking the rest of the day off, starting right now!'

'Rachel, don't…'

'Don't what?'

'Don't resign,' he said wearily.

'Too late,' she snapped, and Justin winced. 'And please don't pretend this isn't what you want. You've been working towards this moment ever since you woke up yesterday morning and found me in your bed.'

Justin could not deny it.

'I'm beginning to wonder if the same thing happened with your previous girl. Or do you only screw the plain ones?'

'Rachel, I didn't mean t—'

'Yes, you did,' she broke in savagely. 'You screwed me good and proper. But I'll survive. I'm a survivor, Justin McCarthy. Watch me.'

He watched her walk with great dignity out of his office, and he'd never admired her more. But he didn't call her back, because she was right. He had screwed her good and proper. And he wanted to do it some more.

Best she leave before he really hurt her.

Best he crawl back into his celibate cave, and best he go back to work!

Rachel felt tears begin to well up in the lift ride down to the lobby. Her anger was swiftly abating and in its place lay a misery far greater than she had anticipated. At the heart of her dismay lay the fact she'd really liked Justin. And she'd really liked working for him.

And you *really* liked having sex with him, came another quieter but more honest voice. That's why you're feeling so wretched. All your silly female attempts to look attractive for him this morning were a big waste of time. You vowed you'd never get that horrible sewing machine out again and what did you do last night? Hauled the damned thing out of the bottom of the wardrobe and worked till midnight practically remaking this wretched suit.

And what did he do? Hardly looked at it, or at you. He doesn't want you any more. He never really did. How could you possibly have started imagining he might? You were just there, when he needed sex. He said as much yesterday. And now you're a nasty reminder of behaviour he'd rather forget.

Rachel's eyes were swimming by the time the lift doors opened, so she fled to the ladies' room in the lobby and didn't come out till she was dry-eyed and back in control.

But she no longer felt like shopping for clothes. What did it matter what she wore around Justin?

Hooking her black carry-all over her shoulder, she headed for the exit. Straight home, she decided.

'Rachel!' a male voice shouted, and her heart jumped. 'Wait.'

Her heart began to race as she turned.

But it wasn't Justin hurrying towards her across the lobby.

It was Eric.

# CHAPTER TEN

'ERIC!' Rachel exclaimed, startled. 'What…what are you doing here?' Possibly a silly question when he'd always worked in the Central Business District in Sydney. It was inevitable that one day, now she was working in the city, she might run into him.

But to run into him only three days after running into him on the Gold Coast seemed to be stretching coincidence too far.

'I was looking for you,' he explained. 'I asked around about your boss and found out he worked in this building.'

'How enterprising of you,' she said coolly.

'I am, if nothing else, enterprising,' he returned, and smiled what she'd once thought of as such a charming smile.

She no longer thought anything about Eric was charming.

She no longer thought he was all that gorgeous, either, despite his grooming still being second to none. His sleek black business suit would have cost a fortune. And he would have spent half an hour blow-drying his hair to perfection this morning. It must be killing him, she thought a bit spitefully, to find that it was receding at a rapid rate.

'Why were you looking for me?' she asked in a less than enthusiastic tone.

'I was worried about you.'

She could not have been more surprised if he'd proposed marriage.

'Good lord, why?'

'Can we go somewhere and talk in private? There's a coffee shop just off the foyer facing the street. How about in there?'

She shrugged with seeming indifference. 'If you insist.'

He didn't enlighten her till the coffee arrived, and she refused to press, despite being curious. The days when she'd hung on Eric's every word had long gone.

'You didn't come to the dinner on Saturday night,' he began, throwing her slightly. What to say to that? Rachel cast her mind back to the night in question and decided to go with the fiction Justin had created.

'We had no need after my boss met with his client.'

'Mr Wong decided against Sunshine Gardens?'

Rachel maintained her cool. 'You don't honestly expect me to discuss my boss's business with you, do you? If that's why you've come, to pump me for inside information for your girlfriend, then you've wasted your time. *And* the price of this coffee.'

'That's not the reason,' Eric said hastily when Rachel made to rise. 'I came to warn you. About your boss.'

Rachel sat back down, blinking. 'Warn me. About *Justin*?'

'Look, I know I hurt you, Rachel. I'm not a fool. The way you look at me now…you probably hate my guts and I can understand that. But I don't hate you. In fact, I think I made a big mistake breaking up with you. You are one special lady and you deserve better in life than getting tangled up with the likes of Justin McCarthy.'

Rachel opened her mouth to deny any involvement with Justin, but after their performance on Saturday night it would be difficult to claim they weren't lovers. Not that it was any of Eric's business who she slept with.

'I don't know what you're talking about,' she said stiffly. 'Justin is a wonderful boss, and wonderful in every other way. What could you possibly be warning me about where he's concerned?'

Eric laughed. 'I have to give him credit. He puts on a good act. But he's not in love with you, Rachel. He's just using you.'

'How kind of you to tell me that,' she said, struggling now to control her temper. 'Might I ask what right you have to say that, what evidence? Or is it just that when you look at me you see a pathetic, foolish woman that no man could really love?'

'There's nothing pathetic or foolish about you, Rachel, and you know it. You're still as beautiful and bright as you always were. But you do have one fatal female flaw. You fall in love with bastards.'

'I am *not* in love with my boss,' she denied heatedly.

But when Eric's eyes searched hers she felt her face flame.

'I hope not,' he said. 'Because he's one bitter and twisted guy. Not that he doesn't have a right to be. I'd be bitter and twisted if my wife did to me what his wife did to him.'

Rachel's mouth went dry. 'What…what did his wife do?'

'I thought you wouldn't know about that. It's not the sort of thing a man would spread around. Charlotte didn't put two and two together on Saturday night when you first introduced him. After all, his is not such an unusual name. But she got to thinking about it last night and made some discreet enquiries, and bingo, he was the one all right.'

'Eric, would you kindly just say what it is you've come to say?'

'Your boss's ex-wife has been Carl Toombs' personal assistant for a couple of years now. And I mean *very* personal. He pays for her apartment and she travels everywhere with him. Their relationship is a well-kept secret but that's the reason she left her husband, to shack up more often with her high-profile boss. You do know who I'm talking about, don't you?'

'Yes, of course I do,' Rachel snapped. 'I might have been out of the workforce for a few years, but I wasn't dead. I don't know of anyone in Australia who wouldn't know who Carl Toombs is.'

'OK, OK, don't get your dander up. Anyway, Toombs is Charlotte's client, the one who wants to buy Sunshine Gardens. Because of their business association, Charlotte's had quite a bit to do with his beautiful blonde PA over the past few weeks, and you know girls. They like to chat. Anyway, the ex-Mrs McCarthy confided in Charlotte over lunch and a few Chardonnays the other day. Apparently, darling Mandy is still suffering great gobs of guilt over her ex-hubby. She told Charlotte how cut up he was when she left him. She confessed she said some pretty dreadful things so that he would hate her and forget her, but that *she'd* never forget the look on his face when she told him she'd been having sex with Toombs for some time. She said she did love her husband and he was mad about her, but she simply couldn't resist Carl's advances. She said Carl wanted her and nothing was going to stop him having her. She said she thinks she broke her husband's heart.'

Rachel didn't say a word. She was too busy absorbing the full ramifications of Eric's news.

'From what I gather he's one very bitter man,' Eric went on. 'Knowing you, Rachel, you probably think he's in love with you. You're not the type of girl to jump into bed idly. But it's not love driving your boss these days. More like revenge.'

'You don't know what you're talking about, Eric. For one thing, I'm not in love with Justin. And I don't imagine for one moment that he's in love with me.'

Eric frowned. 'Then…what is it between you two?'

'That's my business, don't you think?'

'You are sleeping with him, though.'

'That's my business, too.'

'Look, I've only got your best interests at heart, Rachel. I care about you.'

She laughed. 'Since when, Eric? Are you sure you didn't seek me out today to tell me this because you're getting bored with Charlotte and think you might have a bit more of what you once used to take for granted?'

'I never took you for granted, Rachel. I loved you in my own way. I just couldn't see our marriage working with you becoming a full-time home carer. I'm a selfish man, I admit. I wanted more of your time than that. I need a wife whose first priority is me.'

'Then you chose a strange partner in Charlotte. Her first priority is her career. And her second priority is herself.'

'I always knew that. Why do you think I didn't marry her? It was you I wanted for my wife, Rachel. I still do…'

'Oh, please. Spare me. Thank you for the coffee,'

she said, rising without touching a drop. 'And thank you for your very interesting news. You might not know this but you did me a huge favour in telling me about Justin's ex. It's made everything much clearer.' Which it had. She might not know the full details of Justin's thoughts and feelings. But it wasn't revenge driving him. Revenge would have acted very differently at the weekend, and today. Revenge *would* have used her.

Rachel walked away from Eric without a backward glance, her mind wholly and solely on Justin. Alice hadn't exaggerated. Her son's wife certainly was a cold-blooded bitch. Either that, or terribly materialistic and disgustingly weak.

He was better off without someone like her in his life. The trouble was…did he realise that yet?

Maybe. Maybe not. Clearly, he'd been deeply in love with this Mandy. Possibly, he still was. It was hard to say.

Still, time did heal all wounds. Just look at herself. She'd once thought the sun shone out of Eric. She'd been devastated by his dumping her. Today, she hadn't turned a hair at his declaring he still wanted her as his wife. The man meant nothing to her any more, and being free of him felt marvellous.

Rachel suspected, however, that Justin was not yet free of his ex. His beautiful blonde ex, Eric had said. Naturally, she would be beautiful. *Very* beautiful. Men like Carl Toombs didn't take ugly women as their mistresses. They chose exquisite creatures with perfect faces and figures, women with a weakness for money and a fetish for the forbidden.

It was no wonder Justin had an aversion to sex in the office. Rachel understood completely. But it was time for him to forget the past and move on, as she had decided to do.

Of course, she'd had four years to come to her present state of heart and mind. Justin's wife had betrayed and abandoned him much more recently. Only two years ago. And she'd said truly dreadful things to him, according to Eric.

What kind of things? Rachel wondered during the lift ride back up to the fifteenth floor. Had she criticised his skills in bed? Hard to imagine that. Justin left Eric for dead as a lover. And every other boyfriend she'd ever had. Perhaps the wretched woman had told him he wasn't rich enough, or powerful enough? Who knew?

Rachel didn't dare ask him, but she dared a whole lot more. She dared to go back and tell him she'd changed her mind about resigning. She dared to stay. And she dared to go after some more of what they'd shared on Saturday night.

If truth were told, she couldn't stop thinking about it. Surely he had to be thinking about it, too. Rachel could be wrong but she suspected she was the first woman Justin had had sex with since his wife left him.

The thought amazed, then moved her to anger. Selfish people like Eric and Mandy had a great deal to answer for. But you couldn't let them get away with trampling all over your emotions, and your life. You had to stand up and fight back. You had to stop playing the victim and move on. There were other people out there. Other partners. But you had to be open to finding them. You had to embrace new experiences, not run away from them.

Rachel left the lift at her floor and hurried along to her office, her new-found boldness waning a little once she approached the door she'd slammed shut less than an hour ago. Suddenly, she was biting her bottom lip and her stomach was churning. Was Justin still there behind that door, sitting at his computers, slaving away? Probably. It wasn't lunch time yet, and her boss had no reason to go home. He had nothing in his life except his work, a bruised ego and a broken heart.

Till now, that was. Now he had *her*. Her friendship and companionship. Her body too, if he still wanted it.

Her hand was shaking by the time she summoned up enough courage to knock. But it was a timid tap. Annoyed with herself, she didn't knock again. Instead she turned the door knob and went right in.

'Oh, no,' she groaned, her gaze darting around Justin's empty office.

Rachel was battling with her disappointment when she heard a banging noise coming from inside one of the adjoining rooms, the one with the bar and the sofa in it. Before her courage failed her again she marched over and flung open the door.

Justin almost dropped the ice-tray he was holding. He hadn't expected to see Rachel again. Not that day, anyway. After she'd left he'd tried to work, but he'd been too distracted, and too depressed to concentrate. In the end, he'd come in here in search of some liquid relaxation.

'What on earth do you think you're doing?' she threw at him.

Her accusing tone—plus her unexpected reappearance—didn't bring out the best in him.

'What does it look like I'm doing?' he countered belligerently. 'I'm getting myself some ice to put in my Scotch. But the bloody stuff's stuck.'

'But…but you never drink during the day!'

'Actually, you're wrong there,' he said drily. 'I often drink during the day. Just not usually during the week.' He gave the ice-tray another bang on the granite bartop and ice cubes flew everywhere.

'Don't do that!' he roared at her when she hurried over and began picking up the ice cubes. Damn it all, the last thing he wanted was for her to start bending over in front of him.

She ignored him and picked them up anyway, giving him a good eyeful of her *derrière*-to-die-for. 'You shouldn't drink alone, you know,' she said as she straightened and dropped several cubes into his glass.

'What do you care?' he snapped, irritated by her presence beyond belief. 'You're not my keeper. You're not even my PA any more.'

'I am, if you still want me to be. I came back to tell you I don't want to resign. I want to keep working for you.'

He laughed. 'And you think that's good news? What if I said I don't want you working for me any more? What if I said your resigning was exactly what I wanted?'

'I don't believe you.'

'She doesn't believe me,' he muttered disbelievingly, and quaffed back a mind-numbing mouthful of whisky. 'So what do I have to say to *make* you believe me?'

'There's nothing you can say,' she pronounced, and gave him one of those defiant looks of hers. Damn, but she had a mouth on her. What he wouldn't like her to do with it!

He tossed back another decent swig and decided to shock her into leaving again.

'What if I told you that since Saturday night whenever I look at you I'm mentally undressing you? What if I confessed that after you made that joke about you not wearing any underwear it became my favourite fantasy, you not wearing any underwear around the office? What if, when you accused me of having screwed you good and proper, my first thought was that I hadn't screwed you nearly enough?'

She just stared at him, clearly speechless.

'That's only the half of it,' he went on after another fortifying swallow of straight Scotch. 'When you brought me that coffee this morning after Guy left it wasn't coffee I wanted from you but sex. I wondered what you'd do if I asked you to lock the door and just let me do it to you right then and there across my desk. From behind,' he added for good measure.

Her eyes grew wider but she still hadn't said a word. She seemed rooted to the spot, frozen by his appalling admissions.

The trouble was, giving voice to his secret sexual fantasies about her had also had the inevitable effect on his body. Or was it just her, standing there in front of him, within kissing distance?

'Well? What *would* you have done?' he demanded to know, his raging hormones sparking more recklessness.

She finally found her tongue. 'I...I don't know,' came her astonishing answer.

'What do you mean, you don't know?' he shot back, floored by such an ambiguous reply.

'I mean I don't know. I was angry with you back then. Why don't you ask me now?'

My God, she meant it. She actually meant it.

His hand tightened around his glass and his head spun. So that was why she'd come back, was it?

Because she wanted him to seduce her again. He'd suspected this might be the case when she'd come in this morning looking good enough to eat, but he'd been hoping he was wrong.

Any hope of that, or that he could keep resisting temptation disappeared as swiftly as the rest of his Scotch. Emptying the glass, he banged it back down on the bar-top and faced his nemesis.

'Would you go and lock the door, Rachel?' he asked in a gravelly voice. 'Not the one that separates this room from my office. Or the one separating my office from yours. The one out in your office. The one that lets the outside world in.'

She did it. She actually did it. Justin's mind reeled with shock. But nothing could stop him now.

'Now come here to me,' he ordered thickly when she reappeared in the open doorway, looking both beautiful and nervous.

She came, her cheeks flushed with excitement and her eyes glittering brightly.

'I've been wanting to do this,' he growled, and reached up to release the clip. As her hair tumbled down around her face and shoulders Justin knew that he wasn't simply crossing a line here, he was about to propel them both into a world from which there was no turning back, a word where lust ruled and love was nothing but a distant memory. She had no conception of the demons in his mind, or the dark desires that had been driving him crazy since Saturday night. She probably thought he loved her.

Now, that was one transgression he would not be guilty of. Deception. The games he wanted to play with her were sexual, not emotional.

'You do realise I don't love you,' he said as he flicked open the buttons on her jacket.

'Yes,' she surprised him by admitting, though her voice was trembling and her eyes had gone all smoky.

'I will *never* fall in love with you,' he added even as his hands slipped inside her jacket to play with her breasts through her bra. God, but her nipples were hard. So incredibly hard.

And so was he.

'I…I don't expect you to,' she replied somewhat breathlessly.

'You don't have to do anything you don't want to do,' he told her before his conscience shut down entirely.

'But I want you to,' she choked out.

'Want me to do what?' he murmured as he slipped the jacket off her shoulders and let it fall to the carpet.

'Wh…whatever,' she stammered.

Justin suspected she was too turned on to know what she was saying. He was rapidly getting to the point of no return himself.

For a split-second, he almost pulled back and saved her from herself. And from him. But she chose that moment to reach round and unhook her bra herself. Blood roared into his ears as she bared her beautiful breasts to his male gaze. And then she did something even more provocative. She dropped the wisp of a bra on the floor then reached up and rotated her outstretched palms over her rock-like nipples.

Any hope of salvation fled. He was lost, and so, he realised when he looked down into her dilating pupils, was she.

## CHAPTER ELEVEN

THE phone was ringing when Rachel arrived home that night around seven. She raced to answer it, thinking—no, *hoping*—it might be Justin.

'Yes?' she said as she snatched it up to her ear.

'Rach, I was just about to give up and hang up.'

'Isabel!' Not Justin. Of course not. Silly Rachel. 'What…what are you doing, ringing me on your honeymoon?'

'Oh, don't be silly, Rach. We can't have sex *all* the time.' And she laughed.

Rachel almost cried.

'Not that we haven't given it a good try,' Isabel burbled on. 'I think I've worn him out. The poor darling's having a nap so I thought I'd use the opportunity to give you a call and find out how things are going at home. I've already rung Mum and Dad, so don't start lecturing me.'

'I never lecture you, Isabel. Not any more. The boot's on the other foot these days.'

'You could be right there. But you need lecturing sometimes. So tell me, how's things with your job?'

'Fine,' she said with pretend lightness.

'You still getting along with grumpy-bumps?'

'Justin is not a grumpy-bumps. He's just serious.'

And how, Rachel thought with a shiver, trying not to think about the day she'd spent with him.

'In that case, he's probably not gay,' Isabel pronounced. 'Gay men are never serious.'

133

'Justin is definitely not gay,' Rachel said, her tone perhaps a tad too dry.

'Really? Is that first-hand experience speaking there?' her best friend asked suspiciously.

Rachel decided that some sarcastically delivered truths would serve her purpose much better than heated denial. Because no way could she ever tell Isabel what was going on between herself and her boss. Isabel would be scandalised. She was pretty scandalised herself!

'Yes, of course. Didn't I mention it? He can't keep his hands off me. We've been doing it everywhere. On the desk. In the little-men's room. On the boardroom table. Standing up. Sitting down. Frontwards. Backwards. Haven't tried it upside-down yet. But give it time.'

'OK, OK,' Isabel said, sighing exasperatedly. 'I get the drift.'

No, you don't, Rachel thought with an erotically charged shiver. I'm telling you the shocking truth. 'But let's not talk about me,' she went on hastily. 'Can I know where you went on your honeymoon now?'

'Yes, of course. Hong Kong. And we're loving it. The clothes shopping is fantastic. I've been such a naughty girl. Bought a whole new wardrobe. But you know Rafe. He likes me to dress sexily, and all my clothes at home are a tad on the conservative side.'

Rachel had never thought Isabel's wardrobe at all conservative. Just classy.

'You can have them, if you like,' Isabel offered.

'What? All of them?'

'Everything I left behind. Provided you wear them, of course. That's the deal. You have to wear them. To work as well. It's time you bit the bullet and threw out those dreary black suits. I'm sure your boss could cope. It's not as though any of my old outfits are provocative. You can even have the shoes to go with them. We're the same shoe size.'

'Yes, I know. But are you sure, Isabel?' she asked, amazed by her friend's generosity.

'Positive. Actually, there's nothing in that place that you can't have. Take the lot. Handbags. Jewellery. Make-up. Beauty products. Whatever you can find. I won't be needing any of it.'

'You can't mean that, Isabel. You used to spend a small fortune on all your accessories. As for cosmetics and skin products, both bathrooms here are chock-full of them.'

'And I don't need any of it. Look, I brought everything I really like with me, and that includes my best jewellery. The stuff I left behind is just costume jewellery, bought to go with the clothes I've just given you. You're welcome to whatever you can find. If you don't use them they'll only go to waste. I have a new look now, from top to toe. Speaking of new looks, I've also bought some great maternity clothes for when I begin to sprout. Oh, I can't wait to get home and show everything to you.'

'So when exactly will you be home?'

'Next Saturday week. The flight gets in around midday. I'll ring you when we arrive home at Rafe's place and you can come over that evening for dinner.'

'But you won't want to cook after travelling.'

'Who said anything about cooking? We'll order something in. Is that all right by you?'

'Perfect.' There was no worry that she'd be spending any time with Justin on a Saturday. That was one of the many stipulations he'd made during their marathon afternoon of sex and sin. He wasn't offering her a real relationship. He didn't think it was fair to her to build her hopes up in that regard. Meeting each other's sexual needs was what they were doing. But dating was out. So was going to each other's places. Sex was to be confined to the office, but not till after five in future. Today was an exception.

She'd agreed to stay behind after work for a while every day till they were both satisfied. She'd agreed that he would not take her out to dinner afterwards, or take her home. She'd agreed that they wouldn't see each other at weekends.

In hindsight, Rachel could see she would have agreed to anything at the time.

But she knew, deep down in her heart, that she was skating on thin ice where Justin was concerned. She had underestimated the extent of his broken heart, and the darkness that had invaded his shattered soul. If Eric had hurt her, Justin could very well destroy her. But she felt helpless against the power of her need to have him make love to her as he had today. Primitively. Erotically. Endlessly.

There was nothing she wouldn't agree to to continue their sexual relationship.

'Uh-oh, I'd better go, Rach. The lord and master is stirring. Now, don't do anything I wouldn't do till I get home,' Isabel said happily, and hung up.

'No worries there,' Rachel muttered ruefully as she replaced the phone in its cradle. 'Whatever you're doing with Rafe, I'm doing one hell of a lot more with Justin. Much, much more.'

An image flashed into her mind of her straddled over Justin's lap, her back glued to his chest, her arms wound up around his neck. They were seated on his office chair, their naked bodies fused and beaded with sweat, despite the air-conditioning. He was making a pretext of showing her how his programs worked whilst he idly played with her breasts. If he'd expected her to learn anything, he was sadly mistaken. All she'd learned was that she was rapidly becoming addicted to his brand of sex, and rapidly becoming obsessed with him.

If Isabel thought Rafe's body was great, then she hadn't seen Justin's. She quivered just thinking about how he felt, all over. She couldn't get enough of touching him. And whatever else he wanted her to do.

And he'd wanted her to do everything today. There wasn't an inch of his beautiful male flesh that hadn't enjoyed the avid attentions of her mouth, or her hands. She'd been shameless. Utterly shameless.

Yet shame wasn't her overriding emotion when she thought of the woman she became in his arms. The memory evoked the most intoxicating excitement. Her heart thundered and a wave of heat flushed her skin.

There was no way she could voluntarily give up having sex with Justin. No way she could quit now and get another job. She was his, till he decided otherwise. His to admire and desire. His to have and, yes, to hold.

But never to marry, she reminded herself.

Her heart twisted at this last thought. But that didn't stop her racing down to Isabel's walk-in wardrobe and seeing what was there for her to wear for Justin tomorrow. Something classy but sexy, she wanted, her eyes scanning the long rows filled with outfits, most of them suits in pastel shades. She pulled out a pale blue silk trouser suit, then put it back. Trousers did not appeal. She needed something with a skirt, either long and floaty, or short and tight. Something that would draw Justin's eye and recharge his hormones. She wanted him well and truly fired up by five. She wanted him as desperate for her as she already was for him.

A cream linen suit caught her eye, matched with a mustard-gold camisole. The jacket still had long sleeves but that didn't matter yet. Sydney's weather was still overcast and cool.

She laid it across the bed then rummaged around till she found matching cream shoes and bag. The jewellery box on the dressing table revealed a pearl choker with matching earrings. Not real pearls, of course, but still classy-looking. This time she would put her hair up in a more severe fashion, showing her throat and ears. To compensate, she would wear more make-up, paying particular attention to her eyes and mouth. Rachel knew she had nice eyes. And Justin seemed fascinated with her mouth.

Oh, and she would wear perfume. One of the expensive French fragrances Isabel had always favoured. Rachel had already noticed several not quite empty bottles in the wall cupboard above the main vanity unit. She would experiment with a new one each day and find out which one Justin seemed to like the most, then go and buy herself a bottle.

Stripping down to her underwear, she tried on the cream linen suit, pleased to see that it fitted very well, a surprise, considering she was considerably slimmer around the hips and waist than Isabel. Perhaps Isabel had bought it last year when she'd been dieting. The cami was much too tight around the bust, however, so Rachel took it off, discarded her bra and tried it on again.

With her full breasts settled lower on her chest the top felt less tight, but, as Rachel walked over to check her reflection in the cheval mirror on the back of the wardrobe door, the satin rubbing over her naked nipples had them puckering into pebble-like peaks. She winced at the sight of their provocative outline, which screamed her lack of underwear, plus her constant arousal. Would she dare wear it like this? And would she dare take off her jacket?

Oh, yes, she accepted as another wave of heat flooded her body.

She dared.

She would dare anything after today!

# CHAPTER TWELVE

JUSTIN glanced up at the office wall clock for the umpteenth time that afternoon. Almost five. His pulse quickened at the thought that soon he could abandon any pretence of working and do what he'd been desperately wanting to do all day: have sex with Rachel.

Just the thought of it sent his blood racing through his body.

But then another less happy thought intruded. It was Friday again. For the next two days he would not see Rachel at all; could not thrill to the exquisite anticipation of knowing that at the end of the day she would let him remove all her clothes to draw her naked and trembling into his arms.

Last weekend had been almost unendurable without her. This weekend would probably be worse. Justin resolved to keep her with him later than usual tonight. She wouldn't mind. She enjoyed what they were doing just as much as he did, a fact that soothed his conscience somewhat. If he ever thought that what they were doing together was hurting her in any sense he would have to stop.

But *could* he stop, even if his conscience demanded it? That was the question. He had difficulty at the moment doing without her for two days. The prospect of never having sex with Rachel again was an idea he didn't want to address.

Another glance at the clock showed it was finally five o'clock.

His heartbeat took off.

It was time.

Rachel's head snapped up from her computer with a gasp when Justin wrenched open his office door right on the dot of five. She'd been pretending to herself that she hadn't noticed the time, pretending to be working.

But that was all it was. Pretence. She lived for this moment every day. It was what she dressed for. And undressed for. It was why each afternoon at four-thirty she rose to lock the outside door, then go to the ladies' room to make preparations for just this moment. For the last half-hour she'd been sitting there with her panties stuffed in her top drawer and no underwear of any kind covering her bare buttocks and upper thighs. Stay-up stockings had long replaced her pantyhose. She also rarely wore a bra these days, having quickly grown addicted to the feel of silk linings against her bare skin, plus the aphrodisiacal effect of knowing she was naked underneath her clothes.

Their eyes locked across the room and her surroundings slowly began to recede. Suddenly there was only him, and the way he was looking at her.

'Get yourself in here, Rachel,' he ordered, his impatience echoed in the tightness of his neck muscles.

Her legs felt like lead as she levered herself up from her desk and walked, like some programmed robot, into his office. Yet inside she was anything but a cold-blooded machine. She was all heat and hyped-up nerve-endings. Her head was spinning like a top and her heart was pounding behind her chest wall.

The speed with which he yanked up her skirt then hoisted her up onto his desk punched all the breath from Rachel's body. He was between her legs in a

flash, unzipping his trousers and freeing his rather an-
gry-looking erection. Her body was ripe and ready for
him, needing no foreplay. His hands grasped her hips,
his fingertips digging into her skin as he scooped her
bottom to the very edge of the desk and drove into her
to the hilt. With a grunt of satisfaction he set up a
powerful pumping action, his eyes grimacing shut, his
lips drawing back over gritted teeth. Rachel leant back
and braced herself by gripping the back edge of the
desk, but even so her bottom slid back and forth across
the smoothly polished desk-top.

Something—possibly the fact he hadn't even kissed
her first—got to Rachel, and suddenly she wanted him
to stop.

The trouble was…her body didn't want him to stop.
It had a mind of its own. Frantic for release, it was.
And ruthlessly determined in its quest, pushing aside
any gathering qualms and ignoring the danger warn-
ings. Her libido remained recklessly separated from her
heart as pre-climactic sensations began to build and the
need to come became all-consuming.

Her belly tightened. As did her thighs. Her bottom.
Her insides. He groaned in response to her involuntary
squeezing and then they were both splintering apart,
their cries of erotic ecstasy echoing in the stillness of
the room. His back arched back as he shuddered into
her whilst she gripped the edge of the desk so hard her
fingers went white.

But the spasms of pleasure passed, as they always
did, and this time Rachel came back down to earth with
a terrible thud.

The reality of what they were doing together could
no longer be denied. It was beneath her, carrying on

like this. So why was she settling for such an arrangement? *Why?*

The reason was obvious, she accepted with considerable anguish. The reason had always been obvious, if she'd looked for it. The reason was at this moment still inside her body, his arms wound tightly around her waist, his head resting between her sweat-slicked breasts.

It was then that she started to cry.

# CHAPTER THIRTEEN

'I THOUGHT you said you were never going to take me out to dinner,' she said with curiosity—and something else—in her voice. Was it hope?

Rachel's unexpectedly breaking down into tears after the episode on the desk had jolted Justin out of his selfish desires, and made him take a long, hard look at what he'd been doing. He wasn't a complete fool, or a bastard, even if he'd been acting like one. It didn't take him long to realise that a woman of Rachel's standards and sensitivity couldn't indulge her sexual self indefinitely without her emotions—and her conscience—eventually becoming involved. She claimed she was all right, and that she often cried after she came.

But she never had before.

She'd said through her sobs that she didn't want him to stop, but to continue in the face of her distress was something he simply could not do. He hadn't sunk *that* low.

So he'd comforted her as best he could, then announced that he was starving and couldn't possibly go on till they'd eaten, adding that he didn't want any of the take-away muck they sometimes had delivered to the office. He wanted a decent meal. And decent wine.

Despite a momentary look of surprise, she hadn't made any protest, so he'd booked a table in a nearby restaurant whilst she'd made whatever repairs needed to be made after sex, and retrieved her panties from where she always put them in her top drawer. Fifteen minutes later, here they were, sitting opposite each other at a candlelit table, with Rachel finally giving voice to what was a very fair question over his changing the rules of their arrangement.

He stared across the table at her and thought how lovely she looked in the soft candlelight. The simple mauve dress she was wearing was very classy and elegant. There again, all the clothes she wore to work these days were classy and elegant.

'So I did,' he said quietly. 'But things change, Rachel. I thought it was time we talked.'

Was that panic in her eyes? Or fear? Fear of what, for pity's sake? Of his stopping the sex? Or changing the rules?

Maybe she hadn't been lying to him when she said she was all right. Maybe she liked things the way they were. Maybe she'd become as addicted to his body as he was to hers.

Such thinking threw him. He didn't want her feeling nothing but lust for him. He wanted... He wanted... What *did* he want, damn it?

He wants to call it quits, Rachel was thinking.

Oh, God, she couldn't bear it if he did that. Which was perverse, considering. It should be her telling him that, yes, things *had* changed, and that she wanted out. Out of his office and out of his life.

But she stayed silent and waited for him to say what he had to say, nausea swirling in her stomach at the thought he might not want her any more.

'We really can't go on like this, Rachel,' he said, and a great black pit opened up inside her.

'Why's that?' she said, struggling to sound calm and reasonable whilst her world was disintegrating.

He sighed. 'Look, it's been fantastic. I grant you that. Every man's fantasy come true. But I can see things are in danger of becoming…complicated.'

'In what way? I've done everything you asked.'

He stared at her. 'Yes, you certainly have. Just excuse me for a moment whilst I order the wine.'

She sat there numbly, with Justin and the wine waiter's voices nothing but distant murmurs. Her mind was going round and round and so was her stomach. What was she going to do when he told her it was over? How would she survive?

'Rachel…'

'What?' She blinked, then made an effort to gather herself.

'The waiter's gone.'

'Oh. Yes. So he has.'

'The thing is, Rachel, I don't want to continue with what we've been doing.'

She nodded, her mouth as dry as a desert. 'Yes, I rather gathered that.' Her voice sounded dead. Hollow.

'I want to try something a little more…normal.'

Her head snapped back, her eyes rounding.

'I know I said I didn't want a real relationship with you, and I meant it at the time. And, to a degree, that still holds true. Love and marriage are not on my agenda, so I won't pretend I am offering you any hope of that. But I do want you in my life, Rachel, not just as my PA and not just for the sex. I want to go out with you and, yes, go home with you sometimes. My weekends are terribly lonely. Last weekend was… intolerable.'

'Mine too,' she agreed readily, her spirits lifting with what he was suggesting.

'So I was thinking, if you'd like, that we could try that kind of a relationship.'

She struggled not to cry.

'I...I'd like that very much,' she managed, and found a smile from somewhere.

He smiled back. 'I can't promise not to ravage you occasionally in the office.'

'I won't mind.'

He laughed. 'You're not supposed to say that.'

'What am I supposed to say?'

'*No* might be a good start.'

'You're not much good with no.'

'It's not my favourite word, I confess. Not where you're concerned. But it really isn't right, you know, doing it on my desk. I'm finding it increasingly hard to concentrate on my work.'

'Poor Justin,' she said.

'You don't sound all that sympathetic.'

'I'm not.'

'Would you believe I've actually been feeling quite guilty?'

'Not guilty enough to stop, though,' she pointed out with a wry little smile.

He smiled back. 'No. Not nearly *that* guilty.'

The arrival of the wine gave Rachel a few moments to hug her happiness to herself. Justin might not be offering her the world, but being his special lady friend was a big improvement on the role of secret sex slave.

'This is the best wine,' she said after the waiter left and she took a sip.

'Hunter Valley whites are second to none,' Justin replied, sipping also.

'Can…can I tell Isabel about us?' Rachel asked tentatively. 'She'll be home from her honeymoon tomorrow.'

'If you want to. But I'd rather you didn't mention what we've been up to these past two weeks.'

'Heavens, I wasn't going to tell her about *that*!' she exclaimed.

Rachel doubted Isabel would be shocked as such. But she would be furious. With Justin, for treating her best friend in such a fashion. At least now Rachel would be able to say that she was Justin's proper girlfriend. They might even be able to go out with Rafe and Isabel sometimes as a foursome.

Justin's head tipped to one side as he searched her face. 'You have enjoyed what we've been doing, haven't you, Rachel?'

'How can you ask that?' she exclaimed, blushing now. 'You know I have.'

'And your tears tonight… Did you tell me the truth about them?'

She swallowed, then looked him straight in the face. 'Why would I lie?'

'I was worried you might think you're in love with me.'

'Not at all,' she said without batting an eyelid. And it wasn't really a lie, because she was *sure* she was in love with him. 'I…I confess I was bit upset because you hadn't kissed me first. You just…you know…'

He grimaced. 'You're right. It was unforgivable of me. But I refuse to take all the blame. That perfume you're wearing today should be banned. I just couldn't wait.'

Rachel made a mental note to buy a king-sized bottle

of that one. If she couldn't have Justin's love, she could at least ensure his ongoing lust.

'So when are we going on our first date?' she asked eagerly.

'We're on it now.'

'Oh. Yes. So we are. And where to after dinner?'

'I thought I'd take you home to my place for the night.'

Now Rachel was seriously surprised. When he'd said he would like to come home with her sometimes she'd thought he was still keeping his own place out of bounds.

'If you like, that is,' he added.

'I'd like it very much.'

'I lease a furnished apartment at Kirribilli,' he went on. 'No point in buying a place when I plan on setting up my future business out of the city. I'd like to buy some building with a couple of floors and then I can live above the office. I resent the time I waste travelling to and from work. Not that Kirribilli is all that far from here. Just over the bridge. But you know what I mean. Parking in the CBD is appalling and public transport is the pits.'

'I know just what you mean. I don't mind my train trip too much when I get a seat. But that's not always the case. So what's it like, your place in Kirribilli?'

'Very modern. Very stylish. But a bit on the soulless side. Could do with a spot of colour. Everything's in neutral shades.'

'Sounds like the place I live in. It's all cream and cold. I much prefer warm colours and a cosy, almost cluttered feel to a room. That's why I'd like my own place, eventually, no matter how small. Then I could decorate it exactly as I want, with lots of interesting pictures on the walls, and knick-knacks galore.'

'Sounds like Mum's place. Truly, there's hardly a spare space on the walls, or on any of the furniture. She's a collectorholic. You'll have to come over and see her collection of teapots one day. They fill up two china cabinets all by themselves.'

Rachel blinked her surprise. 'You mean you're going to tell Alice about us?'

'Is there any reason you want to keep our friendship a secret?'

'No. I guess not. But you know mothers. She might start thinking we'll get married one day.'

'I can't worry about what she might think,' he said a bit sharply. 'She should know me well enough to know that is never going to happen. Now, why don't you think about what you're going to order for dinner? The waiter's on his way over.' And he picked up his menu.

Rachel was happy to do likewise, aware that her face had to be registering some dismay over his curt remark that he would never marry her. As much as Rachel tried telling herself that she was pleased with the kind of relationship Justin was offering her, deep down in her heart she knew it was a second-rate substitute for marriage and a family.

Isabel would think her a fool for accepting such a go-nowhere affair. What on earth are you doing, Rach, she'd say, wasting more of your life on another man who's never going to marry you or give you children? You're thirty-one years old, for pity's sake. Soon you'll be thirty-two. Grow up and give him the flick. And get yourself another job whilst you're at it.

Easier said than done.

Love made one foolish. And eternally hopeful.

Even whilst cold, hard logic reasoned she *was* wasting her time, Rachel kept telling herself that maybe, one day, Justin would get over his ex-wife and fall in love with her. Maybe, if she was always there for him, he'd wake up one morning and see what was right under his nose. A woman who loved him. A woman who would never leave him. A woman who'd give him a good life. And children, if he liked.

He would make a wonderful father, she believed. And she…she would dearly love the chance to be a wonderful mother.

'So what do you want?' he asked, glancing up from the menu.

You, she thought with a painful twist of her heart. Just you.

## CHAPTER FOURTEEN

RACHEL woke mid-morning to the sun shining in the bedroom window and the smell of fresh coffee percolating. Justin's side of the bed was empty, but she could hear him whistling somewhere.

He sounded happy. And so was she. Relatively.

Spending last night in his bed had given her some hope that Justin hadn't changed the rules of their relationship just so he could have more of what he'd been having at the office. When he'd brought her back to his apartment after dinner he'd been incredibly sweet, and his lovemaking incredibly tender. He'd held her in his arms afterwards, stroking her hair and back. Strangely, she'd felt like crying again at the time, but she'd kept a grip on herself, thank the lord. Justin wouldn't have known what to make of that. She'd finally fallen asleep and here she was, totally rested and...totally surprised.

'Goodness, breakfast in bed!' she exclaimed as a navy-robed Justin carried one of those no-spill trays into the room.

Sitting up, she pushed her hair back from her face and pulled the sheet up around her nakedness just in time for him to settle the tray down across her lap.

'My, this is lovely,' she murmured, eyeing the freshly squeezed orange juice and scrambled eggs on toast, along some fried tomato and two strips of crispy bacon on the side. 'I usually only have coffee and toast. So what are you having?'

'I've already had it,' he said, sitting down next to her on the side of the bed then leaning across where her legs were lying under the bedclothes.

He looked marvellous, she thought, despite the messy hair and dark stubble on his chin. His vivid blue eyes were sparkling clear, with no dark rings under them. He must have slept as well as she had.

'I'll bet you didn't have anything as decadent as this,' she chided.

'I surely did. And I enjoyed every single mouthful. I'm going to enjoy watching you eat yours, too. You need a bit of fattening up, my girl.'

'Oh? You think I'm too thin?' she asked, that dodgy body image raising its ugly head again.

'Not unattractively so, as I'm sure you are aware. But you don't have anything much in reserve.'

'But if I put on weight I won't fit into my lovely new wardrobe. And my boobs will start sprouting. That's where fat always goes on me first.'

'Nothing wrong with a bit more weight on a woman's boobs. Though yours are already a gorgeous handful. Pity any extra weight I gain doesn't go where it would do me the most good. It usually becomes entrenched around my middle.'

'How can you say that? You don't have an extra ounce of fat on you.'

'You didn't see me eighteen months ago. I was the original couch potato with a sprouting beer gut.'

'I don't believe you. You have the best body I've ever seen on a man in the flesh, with a six-pack to envy. And you certainly don't need any extra inches in that other department. You have more than enough for me.'

His laugh carried a dry amusement. 'Being with

someone like you seems to have made a permanent difference to the size of my equipment.'

'So I noticed. But you know what they say. Size doesn't matter. It's what you can do with it that counts. And I certainly have no complaints over what you do with yours.'

'So I noticed. You are seriously good for my ego, do you know that?'

As opposed to his ex-wife, Rachel guessed. Justin's revelation about being a bit overweight and less than fit eighteen months ago gave rise to the speculation that the vain puss he was married to might have criticised him over his physical appearance, as well as his sexual performance. Rachel recalled Justin once implying he thought himself staid, and boring. Had that woman undermined Justin on every level, simply to excuse her own disgusting and disloyal behaviour?

More than likely. Guilt in a human being often searched for any excuse for their own appalling actions.

As much as Rachel understood how such criticisms would have been crushing, Justin must surely now know the woman never really loved him. True love wasn't based on superficial things like gaining—or losing—a few wretched pounds. Or on knowing every position in the Kama Sutra.

Again, she wanted to ask him what Mandy had actually said when she left him, but once again this wasn't the right moment. Hopefully, in time, he might confide in her himself. Meanwhile, she had to play a waiting game.

Wrapping the sheet more firmly around her bare breasts, she tucked into the breakfast whilst Justin watched her with a self-satisfied smirk on his face.

'You're really enjoying that, aren't you?' he said and she nodded, her mouth full of egg.

'I'm brewing some very special coffee for afters.'

She swallowed the last mouthful of egg and smacked her lips. 'If it tastes half as good as it smells, I'll be in heaven.'

'That's what I was thinking about you all yesterday,' he said drily, and she laughed.

'I aim to buy a really big bottle of that perfume this very day.'

He groaned. 'Sadist.'

'Takes one to know one. Now you know how I've been feeling every day in that office, waiting for five to come round. Only a sadist would make a rule like that.'

'Trust me, it was much harder for me, with the emphasis on "harder". Hopefully, we might both have a bit more control at work if we spend every night together.'

Rachel blinked her surprise. '*Every* night?'

'Too much for you?'

She wanted to say no, of course not. But she didn't want to be that easy. She'd been far too easy with Justin so far. Men never appreciated women who were easy.

'Yes, I'm afraid so,' she said. 'We women do have personal things we have to do sometimes, you know. Also, once Isabel gets back I will want to spend some time with her. She's my best friend, after all. Actually, I'm having dinner with her and her husband tonight. Her husband, Rafe, has a terraced house in Paddington. He's a photographer.'

'I see,' Justin muttered, his face falling.

Rachel decided that faint heart never won fat turkey.

'You can come too, if you like,' she said, and was rewarded with a startled smile.

'Seriously?' he asked.

'Of course. There's no way I'm going to be able to keep you a secret from Isabel. I wouldn't even try.'

'But won't she mind having someone extra thrust upon her on such short notice?'

'No, and she's ordering food in anyway.'

'I would have thought she'd be too tired to entertain on the first night back from an overseas honeymoon.'

'I said much the same thing to her on the phone but she insisted. I guess it's not all that long a flight from Hong Kong and I dare say they'll have flown first class. Probably slept all the way. But I'll check with her when she calls me. Which reminds me, I will have to go home this morning to await her call and get fresh clothes.'

'I'll drive you,' he offered.

'Gosh, you mean you have a car?' she teased. 'I thought you lived in trains and taxis.'

He certainly did have a car, a nice new navy number. Not overly flash; more of a family car, with easily enough room for two adults and two children.

Rachel wished she'd stop having such thoughts about Justin, but it was impossible not to dream.

They pulled up at the town house in Turramurra shortly after one, Justin accompanying Rachel inside as she knew he would. And they ended up back in bed, as she knew they would. So much for her resolve not to be easy! But it was so hard to resist him once he started kissing her. They were still in bed together when Isabel's call came shortly after three p.m.

'Yes?' Rachel answered in a slightly croaky voice.

'Rach, is that you?' Isabel asked, sounding doubtful.

'Yes, yes, it's me. Justin, stop that,' she hissed under her breath. 'I have to talk to Isabel.'

'Is that the TV on in the background, or are you talking to someone?' Isabel asked.

'I…um…I'm talking to someone.'

'Oh? Who?' Now she sounded surprised.

Rachel gave Justin a playful kick and he laughed before climbing out of bed and heading for the bathroom, Rachel wincing at the sight of the red nail marks she'd dug into his buttocks. Truly, she'd turned into a wild woman in bed!

'Sounds like a man,' Isabel said.

'It is.'

'Oh, my God, you've gone and got yourself a boyfriend!'

'You could be right.'

'Who? Rafe, Rafe, Rachel's got herself a man!' she called out before returning her attention to her friend. 'Where did you meet him? What's he like? Have you been to bed with him yet?'

Rachel had to smile. Trust Isabel to get down to the nitty-gritty straight away. 'I met him at work. He's gorgeous. And yes, I've been to bed with him.'

'Oh, wow, this is such great news. How old is he?'

'Early thirties.'

'Presumably, he works for AWI.'

'Yes.'

'What's he look like?'

'Tall, dark and handsome.'

'What's he like in bed?'

'Makes Eric look like a moron.'

'Single or divorced?'

'Divorced.'

'Oh. Pity. But you can't have everything, I suppose. So, does Casanova have a name?' she added.

Rachel's stomach swirled. This was going to be the sticky part. 'Um…Justin McCarthy.'

Dead silence at the other end for at least ten seconds. Hearing Justin switch on the shower was a blessing. He wouldn't be returning for a while. Time enough, hopefully, to smooth things over with Isabel.

'Justin McCarthy,' Isabel finally repeated in her best I-don't-believe-you-could-be-such-an-idiot voice. 'Your boss. You're sleeping with your boss. Your obviously not gay but pathetically paranoid boss.'

'Um… Yes.'

'But why? How? *When,* for pity's sake?'

Rachel did her best to explain the circumstances leading up to their first going to bed together, as well as where their affair had gone since then, without it all sounding as though she was desperate and Justin was simply using her for sex.

Her friend's sigh told it all. 'You are just setting yourself up for more hurt, love,' Isabel said.

'Maybe. Maybe not. Either way, it's my choice.'

Isabel sighed. 'True.'

'He's really a very nice man.'

'I suppose I'll have to take your word for that.'

'No, you don't. If you'll let me bring him over to dinner tonight then you can judge for yourself.'

'What a good idea,' she said in a tone that worried the life out of Rachel.

'Promise me you won't say anything sarcastic.'

'Who? *Me?*'

'Yes, you, Miss Butter-wouldn't-melt-in-your-mouth. You've got a cutting tongue on you sometimes.'

'I'll do my best to keep it sheathed.'

'You'd better.'

'Where is lover-boy at the moment?'

'In the shower.'

'Good, because I have something I want to say to *you*.'

Rachel rolled her eyes. Here it comes. 'What?'

'Now, don't take that tone with me, Missy. Someone has to look after your best interests and that someone is me. I know you, Rach. You probably think you love this man. But I seriously doubt it. It's just a rebound thing after running into Eric like that. You've also been very lonely. And loneliness can make a girl do incredibly stupid things. From the sound of things, your boss has been very lonely too, not to mention having had the stuffing kicked out of him. Not too many men could come through an experience like that without a seriously damaged soul. How do you know he's not living out some sort of sick revenge, doing to you what he imagines Carl Toombs is doing to his wife? Have you thought of that?'

'Yes.'

'And?'

'It doesn't fit his character. He's too decent for that.'

'Decent! Reading between the lines, he's been screwing you silly all over your office. I haven't forgotten that little joke you made during our last phone call. Only that wasn't a joke, was it? That was the truth!'

'Sort of. But things have changed.'

'Huh. He's just changed the scene of his crimes, that's all. He's probably afraid you'll slap a sexual-harassment suit on him if he keeps doing it on his desk. He's thinking ahead.'

'Thinking ahead to what?'

'To that day when he gets bored and gives you the bullet.'

'He's not like that.'

Isabel groaned. 'You *do* think you love him.'

'I do love him, OK? So shoot me.'

'For pity's sake, girl, it could just be lust, you know. Even on *your* part.'

'Like it was on yours? With Rafe?'

'That was different.'

'How?'

'It just was.'

'Wait till you meet Justin. Then tell me if you still think that.'

'All right. I will!'

# CHAPTER FIFTEEN

'I STILL can't believe it,' Isabel said to Rafe as the returned honeymooners made the after-dinner coffee together in the kitchen.

'What can't you believe, darling? That you've come back home to find Rachel looking utterly gorgeous and glowing? Or that her creep of a boss—the one you've been ranting and raving about all afternoon—is actually a genuinely nice guy?'

'Both. Frankly, I don't know what to think any more. If I didn't know Justin McCarthy's history I'd say he just might be in love with her. The way he looks at her sometimes... As for Rachel, I've had to abandon any desperate hope I was clinging to that she might only be in lust with the man. She's obviously mad about him.'

Rafe glanced over the kitchen island at the woman *he* was mad about. 'Then why are you still so worried?' he said.

'I just couldn't bear to see her get hurt again. She's had such a rotten deal in life so far, Rafe. She deserves to be happy.'

'I know, sweetheart,' Rafe said soothingly. 'I know. But she's a grown woman. She has to make her own choices and decisions in life. You can't make them for her. Even if you could, what would you say? Leave him before he leaves you? You saw for yourself the physical transformation in her. Whatever happens between them in the end, that can't be a bad thing.'

161

'No... No, you're right. If nothing else, falling for Justin McCarthy has done wonders for Rachel's looks. It's difficult to believe she's the same girl who was worried about having a bit of red dye put in her hair three weeks ago today. I wonder what Alice makes of all this.'

'Alice?' Rafe frowned.

'Justin's mum. She was the one who got Rachel the job as Justin's PA in the first place.'

'Aah, yes. I remember now. Well, maybe Alice doesn't know that her son's new Girl Friday has been promoted to Girl Saturday and Sunday as well.'

'If she doesn't then that would be telling, don't you think? You told your mother about us quick smart. Maybe I'll try to find out over coffee.'

'Isabel,' Rafe said sharply. 'Don't interfere.'

'But...'

'No buts, darling, except butt out. It's their life.'

'Oh, don't be so typically male! The trouble with you is you don't really care. Rachel's not *your* best friend.'

'No. She's not. Which is possibly why I'm a better judge of what you should and shouldn't do. Now, let's take this coffee out to our guests and finish this very pleasant evening chatting about non-inflammatory subjects.'

'Such as what?'

'How about Rachel's new look? That should keep you two girls going till after midnight, talking about hair and make-up and clothes.'

'Very funny.'

'Justin and I could discuss manly things, such as money and football and sex.'

'You're a male chauvinist pig, Rafe St Vincent.'

'Not at all. Just a typical male, as you so cleverly pointed out. And, speaking of typical males, I wonder if Rachel would consider accidentally on purpose getting pregnant to the marriage-shy Mr McCarthy. It's amazing how the thought of your own cute little baby-to-be can focus even the most commitment-phobic people.'

Isabel's eyebrows arched. 'Now, that's an idea. But a bit too soon, I think. Though I might mention it to her later on. Trust you to come up with that one,' she finished ruefully.

'All brilliantly successful ideas should be shared. Come along, darling. If we don't get out there with this coffee, it'll be stone-cold!'

Rachel knew Isabel was out there in the kitchen gossiping to Rafe about her and Justin. But nothing her friend could say would stop her from continuing with her relationship with Justin. The more time she spent with him, the more deeply she fell in love with him. And it wasn't just the sex bewitching her. It was definitely the man. He was everything Eric had never been. Kind. Considerate. Caring. And funny, when he wanted to be. She'd been amazed at what a witty conversationalist he'd been over dinner with people he hadn't met before. It was obvious Rafe liked him. And Isabel too, if she'd put aside her personal prejudice long enough to admit it.

'I like your friends,' Justin said whilst they were sitting there at the dining table alone, waiting for the coffee. 'And I like their house,' he added, glancing around the cosy dining alcove which came off the main lounge room upstairs.

'They'll probably buy a bigger place after their baby is born,' Rachel remarked.

'They're expecting a baby?'

'Didn't I say so? I thought I had. Yes, Isabel was already expecting before they got married. But that wasn't why they got married. They planned it that way. Or Rafe did. Actually, Isabel wasn't going to get married at all. But she wanted a baby. Oh, dear, I'm not explaining this very well. It's a bit complicated.'

Justin smiled. 'It sounds it.'

'Let me try to explain it better. Now, let's see…a few months back Isabel decided to have a baby using artificial insemination, then raise it by herself, because she was sick to death of falling in love with Mr Wrong. You know the kind. Not exactly good husband or father material. She'd already tried the idea of marrying with her head rather than her heart, and was engaged to this really nice architect who felt the same way, but two weeks before their wedding he fell head over heels for another girl and called the wedding off. It was around this time—only a couple of months back really—that Isabel met Rafe. He was going to be her wedding photographer. Right from their first meeting, she was very attracted to him. No, that's understating things. She fancied him like mad. So much so that when she found out he was single and unattached she asked him to go away with her on her pre-booked and pre-paid honeymoon, on a strictly sex basis with no strings attached. Naturally, Rafe agreed.'

'Naturally,' Justin said laughingly.

'Well, yes, what man wouldn't?' Rachel concurred. 'Isabel's drop-dead gorgeous. Anyway, to cut a long story short, Rafe fell in love during their fling and didn't like the idea of Isabel having a baby all by herself. So he set about deliberately getting her pregnant without her knowing, hoping that then she'd marry him.'

'How on earth did he get her pregnant without her knowing it was on the cards?'

'I gather he doctored the condoms.'

'That was an extremely bold move.'

'Love can make you bold, I guess. And wanting something badly enough.'

'I guess,' he said, his eyes clouding over, then drifting off somewhere distant.

'Did you want children when you were married, Justin?' Rachel asked before she could think better of it.

'What?' He stared at her for a second as though he had no idea what she was talking about. But then his eyes cleared. 'Yes, yes, I did. Mandy did, too, till she…' He broke off abruptly. 'Can we discuss something else, please?'

Isabel and Rafe's return with the coffee was a blessing, though Isabel's intuition antennae seemed to pick up on something straight away, and she flicked Rachel a frowning glance.

Rachel gave a little shake of her head and dredged up a covering smile. 'You haven't shown me all the lovely things you bought in Hong Kong yet,' she said brightly.

'I was just saying that to Isabel,' Rafe replied. 'Why don't you two girls take your coffee into the bedroom and do just that? We two men can stay here and talk about man stuff.'

Isabel rolled her eyes as she handed the stylish blue and white mugs of steaming coffee around. 'In that case, you have a deal. Two arrogant, self-opinionated males exchanging macho bulldust is not my idea of a fun time. Come on, Rach, let's get out of here and leave these two to play one-upmanship all by themselves.'

'I'll have you know that I never play one-upmanship!' Rafe called after the girls as they retreated, mugs in hand.

Rachel and Isabel's laughter lasted till the bedroom door was safely shut behind them.

'What happened out there?' Isabel asked straight away. 'You were both happy as larks when Rafe and I left to go make the coffee, and as tense as anything when we came back.'

Rachel sighed. 'The conversation came round to you and Rafe expecting a child and I stupidly asked him if he'd wanted children when he was married.'

'*Stupidly* asked!' Isabel exclaimed, her expression one of outrage. 'What's stupid about a normal question like that? Truly, Rachel, you're not going to turn into one of those women afraid to ask their boyfriend anything about his past. Or your future together, for that matter. I, for one, would like to know *exactly* what his intentions are towards you.'

Rachel had to smile. Dear Isabel. She really was a good friend. When she wasn't playing bossy mother. She didn't know it but she was just like her own mother in some ways, a fact which would pain Isabel if she realised it.

'He wants me to be his lover, his friend and his PA,' Rachel answered patiently. 'But not necessarily in that order of priority. He doesn't want me to be his wife. And obviously not the mother of his children. He doesn't love me. Neither does he want to remarry. He told me so upfront. He's been very honest with me,

Isabel, and I have no right to cross-question him, or try to change the status quo.'

'Oh, Rachel, that's just so much crap.'

'No, it's not. I've gone into this affair with my eyes wide open. I know the score. Justin doesn't want my love. He wants my friendship, my companionship and my body.'

'And you can live with that?'

'For the time being. That doesn't mean I don't have a very different long-term agenda. I'm not that self-sacrificing. I love Justin more than I ever loved Eric and I aim to marry him one day.'

'Wow. Now, that's more like my old Rachel. So what are you going to do? Get pregnant accidentally on purpose after a little while?' Isabel asked excitedly.

Rachel was taken aback. 'Are you insane? That strategy would never work with Justin.'

'How do you know? Rafe said it's a winner if the guy cares about you at all, and you obviously think he does.'

'Yes, I do. But he hasn't totally got over his wife yet. I'm hopeful he will, though, the same way I eventually got over Eric. Time does heal all wounds, you know.'

'No, it doesn't,' Isabel countered sharply. 'Sometimes people get gangrene. On top of that, it took you damned years to get over that rotter, my girl. By the time Justin is ready to move on from his slutty ex, you might be too old to have children. Don't wait, I say. Take a chance and get preggers and see what happens.'

'Uh-uh, Isabel. That worked for you and Rafe because you loved each other. Justin doesn't love me yet. He wouldn't marry me at this point in time and I don't want to be a single mum. I want any child of mine to have it all. Both parents who love him or her, and who love each other.'

Isabel frowned, and cocked her head on one side. 'Are you sure he doesn't? Love you, that is?'

'What? Look, what are you playing at now, Isabel?'

'Just looking at the situation from a different angle. To be honest, if I didn't know Justin's personal history I would have said he was quite besotted with you.'

Rachel could feel herself blushing. 'You really think so?'

'Absolutely. He might very well be in love with you. He just doesn't know it himself yet. Rafe didn't realise he loved me for ages. So tell me one thing. Is Justin going to tell his mother about you, or is your sleeping together to be kept a tacky little secret?'

'Funny you should ask that. I thought he'd want to keep our affair a secret. But no, he's already told Alice over the phone and we're going to her place for lunch tomorrow. Apparently, he has lunch with his mother practically every Sunday.'

'Well, well, well,' Isabel mused. 'That's good news. That's very good news indeed.'

'I thought so too.'

'We have reason to hope, then, don't we?' Isabel said, feeling more optimistic over this relationship than she had all evening.

'We do, Isabel,' Rachel agreed and smiled at her best friend. 'Now, no more talk about Justin. I want to see all the goodies you brought back from Hong Kong.'

# CHAPTER SIXTEEN

'WHAT are you thinking about?' Rachel asked dreamily.

They were in bed together, post-dinner with Isabel and Rafe, post-coitus, both on their backs, both staring up at the bedroom ceiling.

Justin didn't answer immediately, since the truth was out of the question. How could he possibly tell her he was thinking that if she wasn't on the Pill they might have just made a baby together, or, even more amazingly, that he wished that were the case?

Ever since Rachel had told him that story tonight about Rafe deliberately getting Isabel pregnant to get her to marry him, he'd been having the most incredible thoughts. He knew he didn't love Rachel. Hell, how could he when he still loved Mandy? Yet here he was, wanting her to be the mother of his child. And maybe even his wife!

Was he losing his mind? Or had Rachel's also asking him if he'd wanted children when he was married to Mandy made him realise just how much he *had* wanted children? Losing the woman he loved to another man didn't mean he had to lose the chance of having a family of his own, did it?

Another remark of Rachel's tonight came back to tantalise his mind, and torment his conscience.

*Wanting something badly enough can make you bold.*

Would it be bold to tell Rachel he'd fallen in love

with her and wanted to marry her? Or was that just plain bad?

'Justin?' Rachel prompted, but Justin closed his eyes and pretended to be asleep. Better not to answer right now. The lies could wait. Till the time was right.

He heard Rachel eventually sigh, then turn over and go to sleep, but he didn't sleep for quite a while. He was too busy planning his strategy for getting Rachel to fall in love with him.

Taking her to his mother's for lunch tomorrow was an excellent first move. But it would only be the first of many.

Justin hadn't realised till that moment how bold he could be when he wanted something badly enough. Or how ruthless.

'Rachel, my dear!' Alice exclaimed shortly after opening her front door to them. 'I hope you don't take offence but you look simply marvellous! I can hardly believe it.'

Rachel laughed and didn't take offence. 'It's a bit of an improvement from the last time you saw me, isn't it? No more dreary black for starters.' In deference to Alice's suggestion that blue would suit her, she was wearing a blue silk trouser suit that did look very well against her colouring. Her hair had taken ages to do that morning, and so had her make-up, but it was worth it to see the expression of surprise and pleasure on Alice's face.

'And Justin, love,' Alice said, her gaze swinging over to check out her son from top to toe. 'You're looking ten years younger yourself. Whatever you've been doing with Rachel, keep it up.'

'Mum. *Really.*'

'Oh, don't go all prudish on me. You know I can't stand it when you do that. It reminds me of your father, who, might I add, was not in any way prudish behind closed doors. He just liked to act that way in public. Come along, you two. Come through to the back terrace. I've got a nice cold lunch all set out there, with a couple of delicious bottles of Tasmanian wine for us to try.'

'Like father, like son,' Rachel whispered to Justin when he took her arm and guided her down the long central hallway.

'Behave yourself,' he rasped back. 'Or I'll put you over my knee when I get you home tonight.'

She shot him a cheeky look. 'Would you? You promise?'

'Have some decorum,' he said, but smilingly. 'We're at my mother's.'

'What are you two whispering about?' Alice shot over her shoulder.

'I was telling Justin how much I like your house,' Rachel said.

'Which reminds me, Mum. I want you to show Rachel your teapot collection later. She's into pottery and knick-knacks.'

'Oh, wonderful. I'll take her to a few auctions with me. We'll have such fun.'

They emerged onto the sun-drenched back terrace that looked like a new addition to the house, which was federation-style and inclined to be a little dark inside with smallish windows. Cosy, though, from what Rachel had glimpsed during her journey down the hallway. The terrace, however, looked like something that belonged to an Italian villa, with a lovely vine-covered pergola overhead and large terracotta tiles providing an excellent floor for the rich cedar-wood outdoor setting.

The lunch set out on the table looked as if it would feed an army, with all sorts of seafood and salads, and two already opened bottles of white wine resting in portable coolers. The wine glasses waiting to be filled were exquisitely fine, with small bunches of grapes etched into the sides.

'I'll just get the herb bread out of the oven,' Alice said. 'Justin, pour the wine. I don't mean to rush you into eating but a storm's been forecast for this afternoon and I'm worried it might spoil everything. We haven't seen the sun for some time and I wanted to take advantage of it whilst it was there.'

She hurried off, leaving Rachel to openly admire the rest of the huge back yard with its large tract of lawn and neat garden beds along the side and back fences.

'You were lucky to have such a lovely big back yard when you were growing up,' she commented. 'My parents were inner-city apartment people. Career people, too. Frankly, I often felt like the odd man out. I wasn't surprised when they sent me to boarding-school. I was often in their way. Of course, I was upset when they were killed, but it wasn't till I lived with Lettie that I knew the kind of love and attention that a child cherishes. She wanted me. She really did. She was always there when I needed her. I never felt that with my parents. So it was impossible to let her down when she needed me.'

A wave of sadness hit her as she thought of Lettie and the cruel illness that had taken her. She didn't realise Justin was there till he took her into his arms. 'You are the kind of person who would never let any person down,' he said softly. 'A very special person. I am so lucky to have found you, Rachel.' He tipped up her chin and kissed her so tenderly that it brought a lump to her throat.

Was this the kiss of love? Could her heart's desire be coming true this quickly?

Alice clearing her throat had them pulling apart, but Rachel didn't feel at all embarrassed. She was too happy for that. Alice looked happy too. Perhaps she was also hoping for what Rachel was hoping for.

Rachel didn't have the opportunity to find out till after lunch was finished. With Justin retreating to the family room to watch the final round of a golf tournament on TV, Alice was able to draw Rachel into the living room on the pretext of showing her the famous teapot collection. But the conversation soon turned from pottery to personal matters.

'Has he told you about Mandy yet?' she asked quietly.

'He won't speak about her at all. Or his marriage.'

'Typical. His father was like that. Would never speak of emotional matters or past hurts. So, do you really love my son, Rachel? Or is this just an affair of convenience?'

'I love him with all my heart,' Rachel confessed. 'But I daren't tell him that. He told me right at the start he didn't want my love. Just my companionship.'

'Oh, is that what prudes are calling sex these days?' Alice said with a dry laugh. 'Companionship.'

Rachel just smiled. 'I don't dare ask him about Mandy, either. Although I do know who she left him for. It was Carl Toombs. But I don't know why. I can only guess.'

'I see. Well, if he won't tell you what happened then I will,' Alice pronounced firmly. 'That cruel bitch.

There is no other word for her! She told my son that the reason she was leaving him for another man was because he was no longer physically attractive to her. Just because he'd put on a few pounds. At that time he was a dealer, working crippling hours. And slaving away on his own private projects with every spare minute, just to give her the best of everything. When he combined a sedentary job with take-away food and no energy to exercise then of course Justin put on some weight. But he was far from fat. Still, that's what she called him the day she dumped him. Fat and flabby. And boring to boot. She also complained about their sex life, but what time did he have for fun and games when he was beating himself to death making himself rich enough for her? Not that Justin could ever have been rich enough for her, not compared to Carl Toombs. She wanted to justify her appalling behaviour and to do that she sacrificed my son's self-esteem. It was wicked what she did to him that day. Wicked.'

'Poor Justin,' Rachel murmured.

'He was shattered afterwards for a long, long time. His only refuge was in work and exercise. God knows the hell he's been through as a man, emotionally and mentally. I can't tell you how happy I am that he's finally met a decent girl like you, a girl who can truly appreciate the fine man he is. You *do* really love him, don't you?'

'Alice, I'm crazy about him. As for Mandy, she had to be stupid not to appreciate what she had.'

'That's the strange thing. I honestly thought she did. She seemed to love Justin when she married him. And she always said she'd have a baby as soon as they were financially secure. Frankly, when she did what she did I was almost as shocked as Justin. She didn't seem that sort of girl. Of course, she *is* the sort men always made a play for.'

'She's really that beautiful?' Rachel asked, her heart twisting with jealousy.

'I have to admit she's stunning to look at. And she has a captivating manner as well. A real charmer, no doubt about that. I'm not surprised that the likes of Carl Toombs went after her. What did surprise me was that he succeeded in getting her. I honestly thought she loved my son. Obviously, she had us both fooled. Maybe she was always a little gold-digger at heart. Though, to give her some credit, she didn't take a cent from Justin when she left him. Guilty conscience, probably. Though I dare say she was already getting enough money out of her wealthy lover. Mistresses of men like that don't want for anything. Still, if she thought he was going to leave his wife and marry her then she's been sorely mistaken.

'But Justin will marry you,' Alice added, and Rachel's heart jumped.

'Why do you say that?'

'Because he'd be crazy not to. And my son is not crazy. You wait and see. I suppose you haven't told him you love him.'

'No way. Why? Do you think I should?'

'Not yet. Men like to think love and marriage are their idea entirely. It's a male-ego thing. And, speaking of male ego, I think we should rejoin said male ego before it begins to feel neglected.'

Both women were chuckling away when they entered the family room, only to be shushed into silence by said male ego watching male stuff. They looked at each other and pulled appropriate faces, then withdrew to the kitchen to make afternoon tea and exchange the exasperated view that they didn't know why women bothered falling in love with any man in the first place!

# CHAPTER SEVENTEEN

RACHEL insisted Justin drop her off home after the luncheon at his mother's. Without his coming in.

'I have washing to do,' she told him. 'And a host of other little jobs to organise myself for the coming week. I'm sure you do, too,' she added firmly when he looked as though he was going to argue.

He sighed, then went.

The following morning Rachel was so glad she'd taken that stand. Glad she was alone and travelling on the train to work. Very glad she'd got a seat and she could read the front-page story in the daily newspaper privately.

TOOMBS FLEES AUSTRALIA, the headlines screamed. TYCOON IN INVESTMENT SCANDAL.

The details were a bit sketchy, but it seemed Carl Toombs had finally done what many people had forecast for him. He'd gone bust, and taken a lot of creditors and investors with him. The journalist writing the article implied it was only his company that had gone belly-up. On a personal basis, Toombs himself was probably still as rich as Croesus. Being a conscienceless but clever crook, he would have siphoned money off into Swiss bank accounts, or other anonymous offshore establishments, before doing a flit at the weekend, minus his family.

There were photos of his wife and children at the gate of his harbourside mansion, plus the classic comment from the wife saying she knew nothing about her

177

husband's business dealings, and had no idea where he was. She claimed to be as devastated as his employees and business colleagues, who'd all been left high and dry without their entitlements etc etc etc.

Did that include his PA-cum-mistress? Rachel wondered. Or had she vanished with the disgraced tycoon?

Only time would tell, she supposed. But how would Justin react to this news? Rachel couldn't even guess. This was one area where she still didn't have all the answers, despite what Alice had told her the previous day. The subject of Mandy was *verboten* with Justin.

Rachel arrived at work in a state of nervous anticipation over Justin's mood. No use hoping he wouldn't have seen the headlines and read the story. He worked out every morning with people who lived and breathed such news. It would be the main topic of conversation in AWI's gym this morning. It would be the main topic for discussion in just about every office and household in Sydney that day. But not hers. She didn't dare bring the matter up.

Or did she? It wouldn't be normal not to mention it. Oh, she didn't know what to do for the best!

Justin was already in his office when she arrived, with his door firmly shut. She dumped the paper on top of her desk in full view, then set about making his usual mug of coffee, determined to act naturally. When it was ready she tapped briefly on the door then breezed right in, as was her habit these days.

Justin was sitting at his desk with his nose buried in the morning paper.

'So what do you think of Carl Toombs going broke like that?' she remarked casually as she put his coffee down. 'I was reading about it on the train on the way in. The papers are full of little else.'

When he glanced up at her, he didn't look too distressed. Just a bit distracted.

Rachel's agitation lessened slightly.

'Couldn't have happened to a nicer bloke,' came his caustic comment.

'I guess he's not really broke, though,' Rachel remarked. 'People like that never are.'

'Maybe not, but the media will hound him, wherever he goes. He won't have a happy life.'

'I pity the people who worked for him,' Rachel went on, and watched his eyes.

They definitely grew harder. And colder.

'People who work for men like Toombs are tarred with the same brush. If you lie down with dogs, don't complain when you get up with fleas.'

Rachel was shocked by the icy bitterness in his voice. Shocked and dismayed. He wasn't over Mandy at all. Not one little bit.

Her phone ringing gave her a good excuse to flee his office before she said something she would later regret. She was quite glad to close the door that separated them.

It was Alice, who'd seen the news about Toombs on a morning television programme.

'There was no mention of Mandy,' she said.

'No,' Rachel agreed.

'She always did keep a very low profile. How's Justin?'

'Hard to say.' Rachel didn't want to get into the habit of gossiping about Justin to his mother. 'Would you like me to put you through to him?'

'Lord, no. No, I was just wondering. I also wanted to say again how lovely you looked yesterday, Rachel.'

'Thank you, Alice. And let me say that was one fantastic spread you put on. You're sure you weren't try-ing to fatten me up?' she joked just as the door from the corridor opened and the most striking woman Rachel had ever seen walked in. She looked like some-thing you saw in the pages of the glossies. Long blonde hair. Even longer legs. Enormous blue eyes. Pouting mouth. A body straight out of an X-rated magazine.

'Er—Alice,' Rachel went on, trying not to sound as sick as she was suddenly feeling. 'I...I have to go. Someone's just come in...'

Not just *some*one, of course. *The* one. The cruel bitch. The cruel but incredibly beautiful bitch.

'Can I help you?' Rachel asked frostily as hatred warred with fear. It was no wonder Justin hadn't got over her. Who could ever compare with this golden goddess? She was the stuff men's dreams were made of.

Admittedly, she was wearing a tad too much make-up for day wear, especially around her eyes, and she was dressed rather provocatively, if expensively. Her camel suit had to be made of the finest leather—since it didn't wrinkle—but it was skin-tight, with a short, short skirt and a vest top with cut-in arm-holes and a deep V-neckline. Her gold jewellery looked real, though, again, there was a bit too much of it for Rachel's taste. Several chain necklaces, one of which was lost in her impressive cleavage. Dangling earrings. A couple of bracelets on each wrist. Even an anklet, which drew Rachel's gaze down to the matching camel-coloured shoes, along with their five-inch heels.

She looked like a very expensive mistress. Or an equally expensive call-girl.

'I was told this was Justin McCarthy's office,' she said in a voice which would be an instant drawcard on one of those sex phone lines. Low and husky and chock-full of erotic promise. 'Is that right?'

'Yes. And you are…?'

'I'm Mandy McCarthy, Justin's ex-wife,' she informed Rachel without a hint of hesitation. 'And you must be Justin's new PA,' she added with a strange little smile.

Rachel stiffened. 'That's right.'

'I see,' she said. 'Yes, I see. Is Justin in here?' she added, going straight over to Justin's door and winding her long bronze-tipped fingers around the knob.

Rachel was on her feet in a flash. 'You can't just walk in there.'

'You're wrong, sweetie,' the blonde countered, her smile turning wry. 'I can. And I'm going to. Please don't make a scene. I need to speak to Justin alone and I don't have much time.'

'If you say anything to hurt him,' Rachel ground out through clenched teeth, 'anything at all…I'll kill you.'

She laughed. 'You know, I do believe you would. Lucky Justin.' And then she turned the knob and went right in.

Rachel sank back down into her chair, ashen-faced and shaking.

Justin couldn't have been more shocked when the door opened and Mandy came in.

'What the—?' he muttered, automatically rising to his feet.

'Sorry to drop in like this, Justin,' she purred, shutting the door behind her. 'I don't think your girlfriend outside is too happy about it, but that can't be helped. You can tell her after I've gone that I'm no threat to your relationship.'

'Relationship?' Justin repeated, his head reeling.

'Don't bother denying it. Charlotte told me all about you two.'

It took Justin a couple of seconds to recall who Charlotte was.

'I have no intention of denying it,' he said coolly enough, pleased that he'd managed to find some composure.

'She looks very nice,' Mandy remarked and started to sashay across the room towards his desk. 'Much nicer than me.'

Justin couldn't take his eyes off her, the way she was walking, the way she looked. This wasn't the woman he remembered. Mandy had never dressed like this, or walked like that. Why, she looked like a tart! An expensive tart, admittedly. But still a tart.

'I won't take up too much of your time,' she went on in a voice he didn't recognise either. It was all raspy and breathy. 'I have to leave for the airport shortly. I'm joining Carl overseas. Don't ask me where and don't look so surprised. You must have read the paper this morning, and you must have guessed I'd go with him. Mind if I sit down? These high heels are hell. But Carl likes me to wear them. He says they're a turn-on.'

She pulled up a chair and sat down, her skirt so tight she had difficulty crossing her legs. When she did, he had a better view than a gynaecologist. Thankfully, she was wearing panties, though he didn't look long enough to check what type.

Justin sank back down into his chair, stunned. She was misinterpreting his surprise but it didn't matter now. What mattered was that he wasn't feeling what he always thought he'd feel if he crossed Mandy's path again. There was no pain. No hurt. Hell, he couldn't even dredge up any hate! When he looked at this…stranger…sitting across from him, she bore no resemblance to the woman he'd loved. She'd once been a truly beautiful person, both inside and out. Now she was exactly what she looked like: a woman for hire. Cheap, yet expensive. All he felt was confusion, and curiosity.

What did she see in Carl Toombs that she would do this to herself for him?

'Why, Mandy?' he asked. 'That's all I want to know. Why?'

'Why? I would have thought that was obvious, darling. I love the man. It's as simple as that.'

'I don't find that thought simple. One minute you were in love with me and then you were in love with him? What was it about Toombs that you fell in love with? From all accounts, he's an out-and-out bastard.'

She looked uncomfortable for a second. Then defiant. 'He's not all bad. You don't know him the way I do. Sure, he doesn't always play life by the rules, but he's the most exciting man I've ever known. I…I can't live without him, Justin. I'll go wherever he wants me to go; be whatever he wants me to be; do whatever he wants me to do.'

Justin was appalled. The woman was obsessed. But it wasn't a healthy obsession. It was dark, and dangerous, and self-destructive. The wonderful girl he'd loved, and married, was gone forever.

'What exactly are you doing here, Mandy?' he asked, feeling nothing but sadness for her. 'I don't understand…'

'I came here to apologise. In person. The things I said to you the day I left you. I didn't mean them. Any of them. I was just trying to make you hate me as much as I hated myself that day. You'd done nothing wrong and, despite everything, I still cared for you very much. But I...I just *had* to be with Carl.' Tears suddenly welled up in her eyes but she dashed them away. 'Silly me. Crying over spilt milk. What's the point? I am what I am now and nothing will change that.'

'And what are you now?' he asked, still having difficulty taking in the change in her.

Her eyes locked onto his and they were nothing like the eyes he remembered. These eyes had seen too much. Done too much.

Her laugh made his skin crawl. 'I'd show you if I had time, and if your lady friend out there wouldn't have to go to jail for murder.'

'What are you talking about?'

'When I came in just now she told me if I said anything to hurt you again she'd kill me.'

'Rachel said that?'

'That surprises you?'

'Did you tell her who you are?'

'Yes. But she already knew. I could see it in her face. I had the feeling she knew quite a lot about me. *You* didn't tell her?'

'No.'

'Well, she knows everything,' Mandy insisted. 'Trust me on this.'

His mother, he realised with a groan. Yesterday. Or possibly earlier. He shook his head in amazement. 'She never said a word.'

'Women in love will do anything not to upset their man.'

Justin stared at her. Was she right? Did Rachel love him? Dear God, he hoped so.

'Did I tell you how fantastic you're looking, Justin?

How handsome? How sexy? I'm a fool. I know I'm a fool. But my fate is sealed, my darling. Just remember...I loved you once.' She uncrossed her legs and stood up abruptly. 'Marry your Rachel, Justin. Marry her and have children and be happy. I must go,' she added when her eyes filled again. 'I have a plane to catch.'

She was gone as quickly as she'd come, leaving Justin sitting there, staring after an empty doorway. When Rachel filled that doorway he blinked, then saw how worried she was looking.

'It's all right,' he said reassuringly. 'She's gone. For good.'

'But is she really gone for good, Justin?'

He rose, realising that was why Mandy had come. To set him free; free to love again. She'd taken time out from her not-so-good life to do a really good thing.

'Yes,' he said. 'Yes, she's really gone. For good.'

By the time he reached Rachel, she was crying. His heart turned over as he realised she had loved him all along. He drew her into his arms and held her close.

'We're going to get married, Rachel,' he whispered against her hair. 'We're going to work together, buy a home together and have children together. Oh, and one more thing. I love you, Rachel. More than I have ever loved before. Much, much more.'

Two months later, Carl Toombs' yacht was lost in a hurricane near the Bahamas. All on board perished.

Ten months later Justin and Rachel were married, with Rafe as best man and Isabel as matron of honour. Alice minded Isabel's newborn daughter during the ceremony and the baby didn't make a peep. Alice was duly voted by the wedding party as chief babysitter for all their future children and ordered never to sell her large home with its large back yard.

She didn't. And Alice's home was regularly filled with love and laughter for many years to come.

**Modern Romance**™
...seduction and
passion guaranteed

**Tender Romance**™
...love affairs that
last a lifetime

**Sensual Romance**™
...sassy, sexy and
seductive

*Blaze Romance*™
...the temperature's
rising

**Medical Romance**™
...medical drama on
the pulse

**Historical Romance**™
...rich, vivid and
passionate

*27 new titles every month.*

*With all kinds of Romance for
every kind of mood...*

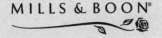

MILLS & BOON®

MILLS & BOON

Helen Brooks
Lynne Graham
Kim Lawrence

# BUSINESS *Affairs*

Three brand-new stories about falling for the boss

## *Available from 17th January 2003*

*Available at most branches of WH Smith,
Tesco, Martins, Borders, Eason, Sainsbury's
and all good paperback bookshops.*

0203/24/MB62

# 2 FREE

## books and a surprise gift!

We would like to take this opportunity to thank you for reading this Mills & Boon® book by offering you the chance to take TWO more specially selected titles from the Modern Romance™ series absolutely FREE! We're also making this offer to introduce you to the benefits of the Reader Service™—

- ★ FREE home delivery
- ★ FREE gifts and competitions
- ★ FREE monthly Newsletter
- ★ Exclusive Reader Service discount
- ★ Books available before they're in the shops

Accepting these FREE books and gift places you under no obligation to buy, you may cancel at any time, even after receiving your free shipment. Simply complete your details below and return the entire page to the address below. *You don't even need a stamp!*

**YES!** Please send me 2 free Modern Romance books and a surprise gift. I understand that unless you hear from me, I will receive 4 superb new titles every month for just £2.55 each, postage and packing free. I am under no obligation to purchase any books and may cancel my subscription at any time. The free books and gift will be mine to keep in any case.

P3ZEA

Ms/Mrs/Miss/Mr ......................Initials................................

BLOCK CAPITALS PLEASE

Surname ................................................................................

Address ................................................................................

..............................................................................................

.............................................................Postcode.................

**Send this whole page to:**
**UK: FREEPOST CN81, Croydon, CR9 3WZ**
**EIRE: PO Box 4546, Kilcock, County Kildare (stamp required)**